PRAISE FOR
THE TEMPTATION SAGA

"Is it hot in here? Congratulations, Ms. Hardt. You dropped me into the middle of a scorching hot story and let me burn."

~ *Seriously Reviewed*

"I took this book to bed with me and I didn't sleep until 4 a.m. Yes, it's that damn engrossing, so grab your copy now!"

~Whirlwind Books

"Temptation never tasted so sweet... Both tempting, and a treasure... this book held many of the seductive vices I've come to expect from Ms. Hardt's work."

~Bare Naked Words

Treasuring AMBER

THE TEMPTATION SAGA
BOOK FIVE

WATERHOUSE PRESS

This book is an original publication of Helen Hardt.

This is a work of fiction. Names, characters, places, and incidents either are the product of the author's imagination or are used fictitiously, and any resemblance to actual persons, living or dead, business establishments, events, or locales is entirely coincidental. The publisher does not assume any responsibility for third-party websites or their content.

Cover Design by Waterhouse Press, LLC
Cover Photographs: Shutterstock

Paperback ISBN: 978-1-943893-30-0
PRINTED IN THE UNITED STATES OF AMERICA

Treasuring AMBER

THE TEMPTATION SAGA
BOOK FIVE

In memory of my grandmother,
Theresa Zeuch Freitag

CHAPTER ONE

"You want me to come to a baby shower? Are you kiddin' me?" Harper Bay paced the length of his father's—now *his*—office in his mother's—now *his*—ranch house.

His little sister's sigh cut right through the phone. "Couples showers are the new thing now, Harp. Amber says—"

"Sheesh, Catie." Harper Bay rolled his eyes, thankful his sister couldn't see him through the phone. He was damn sick of hearing what Amber Cross had to say. That bleached blond manicurist who had become Catie's new soul sister spouted off all kinds of newfangled ideas, and he didn't like a one of them. "Dallas and Annie just had the twins a month ago, and none of us guys had to go to a shower. And you forget one important little detail."

"What's that?"

"Last time I checked, I'm not a 'couple.'"

"Co-ed shower, then. We're talking semantics here." Catie's tone softened. "Don't you want to welcome little Violet?"

How in hell does she do that? Her petal-soft voice never failed to make him wilt. He was a sucker for his baby sister, and he'd be just as much of a sucker for his new niece. Violet was a beauty even at a week old, with a mop of black hair and eyes the darkest sapphire blue. They'd probably turn big and brown like Catie's. She'd be a heartbreaker for sure.

But a baby shower? He was a man, for God's sake. A

damned cowboy. Cowboys did not go to baby showers. That had to be in a rulebook somewhere.

He shook his head. "What's Chad think of this nonsense?"

"Chad says 'whatever makes me happy.'"

Christ.

Whipped.

Harper had known Chad McCray most of his life. A bigger womanizer hadn't existed on the planet...until Catie reeled him in. Now Chad was the epitome of whipped. His face was probably next to "whipped" in the damned dictionary. Harper couldn't prevent a chuckle.

"What are you laughing at?" Catie demanded.

Why not be honest? "Just your whipped hubby, that's all."

"For your information, Chad is *not* whipped."

"Give me a break, Catie-bug. You have the cowboy wrapped around your little finger, and it won't be long till that pretty little daughter of yours has him twisted around hers, too."

Catie's soft laugh gave her away. She knew her husband was whipped. Heck, she was whipped, too. Those two were crazy about each other. Crazy in a way his and Catie's parents had never been. Crazy in a way Harper had never been and probably never would be. He had a ranch to run now. When his father passed away several months ago, Harper had become sole owner of Cha Cha Ranch outside of Bakersville, Colorado. His mother, who'd inherited the ranch when Harper was a boy and transferred it to her husband, still lived in the big ranch house and would for as long as she wished. His uncle, Jefferson Bay, also lived there. Jeff had been estranged from the family for the last three decades, and they were slowly—very slowly—rebuilding their relationship.

Nope, no "whipped" for Harper. He had too much to do. Too many responsibilities. He wasn't sure when he'd last had a date.

How long had it been since he'd had sex?

Too damn long. Had they changed it?

"Harp?"

Reality. Catie. Sometimes the magnitude of owning a whole beef ranch overwhelmed him. "Sorry, just thinking." He sat down in his father's—*his*—chair. "I really think I'll pass on the shower thing, Sis."

"Please? Rafe is coming with Angie. They're coming in from the western slope just to attend."

"They haven't seen Violet yet. They're coming to see her, not for the shower."

"So they'll kill two birds with one stone."

"I suppose they will. I, however, have already seen my beautiful niece, and I plan to see her a lot. Just not during some girly shower."

"It's not going to be a girly shower."

"Oh yeah? You getting a stripper?"

Another sigh from Catie. "Geez, Harp."

"Sorry." Though he wouldn't mind seeing Amber Cross strut her stuff naked. Damn, she had the body of a stripper. Lithe long legs curled around a silver pole, platinum locks falling over rosy-skinned shoulders...pink nipples peeking through...

His groin tightened.

Christ. His body betrayed him. Amber was so not his type. Though she was a Texas native and the reigning Bakersville Rodeo Queen, she was about as far from the girls Harper had grown up with as Maine was from California. Cute Colorado farm girl? *Hell, no.* Nearly white tresses, long red fingernails, leather miniskirts, and sequined tube tops...

Damn, the woman was hot.

Hot, and a major pain in the ass with her couples shower. She'd had Catie doing all kinds of weird crap in the last year. Thursday night happy hour at The Bullfrog had become a tradition for his baby sister. She never missed it, even when she'd been big as a house with Violet. Virgin drinks, yes, but still out on the dance floor shakin' her booty with her new BFF.

He couldn't believe Chad allowed it. Heck, of course he did. The man was so whipped.

"So are you coming or not?"

"You know I love you and I love Violet." He sighed. "But no. I'm sorry."

"Have it your way, then. Everybody else in town will be here."

"Tell everybody else I said hi."

"Fine." Her voice cracked. "Goodbye." Catie's phone clicked.

He didn't want to hurt her, but a baby shower? Sorry, this cowboy wasn't turning in his man card.

★ ★ ★

"Hey, Tom, give me a Fat Tire."

"Comin' up." Tom Grayhawk, the bartender, smiled. "What's eatin' at you tonight?"

"Nothin'." Harper turned and looked toward the door. "Oh crap."

"Now what?"

"Here comes that damn Amber."

Tom chuckled. “Damn Amber? She’s a luscious thing in my book.”

“Hot as hell,” Harper agreed, “but not my type.”

“Hot as hell isn’t your type?” Tom slid a bottle of beer across the wooden counter.

“This particular girl is definitely not my type. Do you know she wants me to—”

“Harper Bay.”

Amber’s voice was low and sultry, like the smoky aroma of aged bourbon. She slid onto the bar stool next to Harper and crossed her long tan legs. The woman was always a light bronze, even now, in springtime. Had to be fake. Her denim miniskirt hardly covered her thighs as she sat. Harper tried not to stare.

“What’ll it be, beautiful?” Tom asked.

“Like you have to ask?” Her long brown eyelashes batted at Tom.

Harper’s jeans seemed tight. He wiggled uneasily on his stool.

“One cosmo comin’ up,” Tom said.

“So,” Amber said.

Harper cleared his throat. “So what?”

“You’ve got your little sister in a dither over this shower thing. She can’t stand the thought of you not being there.”

He let out a huff. “She’ll get used to it. Men don’t belong at baby showers. Why didn’t she have the shower months ago, anyway? Before Violet was born?”

“’Cause she and Chad didn’t want to know the sex. They wanted to be surprised in the delivery room. So I advised—”

“You advised? Another one of your cockamamie ideas?”

She shook her head and rolled her eyes. Totally blowing

him off. Why did that irk him so much?

"I advised her to wait till the baby was born so people could bring gender appropriate gifts. It made perfect sense to Catie. Who wants a bunch of yellow and green baby clothes?"

"Yellow and green?"

"Yes, yellow and green. No one buys blue or pink when they don't know the sex. Everyone knows that."

He smirked. "Pardon me. I missed the lecture on baby shower purchasing etiquette."

Amber pursed her lips. "Was that supposed to be funny?"

"Hardly. None of this is funny from where I'm standin'. I am not going to a baby shower. Case closed."

Tom set the cosmo in front of Amber. "Simmer down, Harp. I'm going. It'll be a great party."

"Am I truly the only guy left in this town who thinks this is an atrocity?"

"I didn't say that, but the baby is your niece. She's my brother's niece. So I'm going to pay my respects. Besides, Chad McCray throws a great party."

"See?" Amber said. "Tom knows what he's talking about. You've really upset Catie. Besides, couples showers aren't anything new. They're all the rage in Texas."

"Well, we certainly want to do everything the way they do in Texas." Harper shook his head. "But last time I checked, I'm not a couple."

"Neither am I," Tom said, "but I'm going. I'm tagging along with my dad and Lilia."

"I'm not a couple either," Amber said. "So what?"

Tom curved his lips upward in a lopsided smile.

Shit. He's up to no good.

"Why don't you two go together?"

Good God in heaven.

Amber would say something, surely. She'd shoot that idea down. The two of them had less in common than Jesus and the devil. Harper waited, tense.

Come on, Amber. Speak. Tell him you'd rather be hung out by your toenails than be my date at some couples shower.

"I'm free if you are," she said coyly.

Christ.

"Well, then, you all have a date." Tom smiled and raised one eyebrow.

Damn it, Grayhawk, I owe you one. "I can't be her date since I'm not going."

There. Still a save.

"No, no, no," Tom said. "This lovely lady needs an escort. And you don't want to disappoint your pretty little sister."

Hitting him right where it hurt. And now he had to take Amber to the party on top of everything else. Either that or reject her right here. Even though they had no interest in each other, he was too much of a gentleman to do that.

He gritted his teeth. "Fine."

Amber winked at Tom and sipped her cosmo. "Perfect. I'll look forward to seeing you. Pick me up at the beauty shop on Saturday at two."

Tom winked back.

Harper downed the last of his beer and plunked the bottle on the bar. *Damn it all.*

He'd just been played like a fiddle.

CHAPTER TWO

"Well, hey there, Harper." Judy Williamson, the owner of the salon where Amber worked, looked up from the head she was blowing dry.

"Hi there."

"I hear you're taking Amber to the party this afternoon. I'm closing up early when I'm done with Lisa, here. We're all heading over."

"Great." Could he be less enthused?

Amber sat in the back of the salon, cleaning up her...was it a desk? What did one sit at to do nails, anyway?

"Hey there," she called. "I'll be with you in a sec."

"No hurry." He sat down and thumbed through a hair styling magazine.

"When are you going to let me play with that gorgeous mane of yours, Harp?" Judy asked as she clicked the blow dryer off.

"Uh...well, I still see Ron over at the barber shop, you know."

"Not often enough. You'll be touching your shoulders in a few more days."

"Works for me."

"You've got a gorgeous head of hair, just like both your sisters and your mom. I love doing all their hair."

I'm sure you do. "Amber, you coming?"

Was the whole world bound and determined to turn him

into a woman this week? First a shower, now Judy wanted to do his hair?

Amber got up from her table and grabbed a bag. "Yes, I'm ready."

Did she have to wear miniskirts all the damn time? The woman had one fine pair of legs, and her curvy little ass stuck out just right. Her platinum hair was pulled into a high ponytail today. She had one sexy neck. Truth be told, she had one sexy everything.

He'd said it before. Amber Cross was hot.

If only she weren't such a gigantic pain in his ass. She and her Texas ways. If Texas was so great, why the hell was she here?

Couples showers. Christ.

"I'm ready, Harper."

Eyes so light brown they were almost gold stared up at him. How had he never noticed her eyes before? They were amber. Amber like her name.

"Yes?" she said.

He blinked. "What?" He inhaled a whiff of lavender. She even smelled good.

"You're looking at me funny."

"Oh, sorry." He eyed a pink gift bag dangling from her wrist. "What's that?"

"My present for the baby, of course. What are you bringing?"

His eyebrows shot up. A present? "Um...I guess I didn't think about it."

"It's a shower, Harper. You *shower* the baby with gifts."

"I'll get her whatever she wants. She's my first niece after all."

"You can't go to this party empty-handed. Come on." She grabbed his hand—he tried to ignore the tingle—and dragged him across the street. "Let's see. What can we find on short notice?"

"I don't need to bring anything. Catie knows I'm good for it."

"Yeah, yeah, yeah. Let's try here." She led him into Terry's gift shop. A froufrou place. Harper had never set foot in there.

"Here." Amber handed him a pink teddy bear the size of a small car. "This'll work."

"Just what every kid needs," Harper said under his breath.

"I heard that. Pick something yourself, then. But we're not leaving here till you buy something for your niece."

Harper chose a stuffed brown horse, chocolate brown just like Catie's favorite mare, Ladybird. Teddy bears were overdone anyway, and Catie would appreciate this more.

"Will this do?"

Amber nodded. "Perfect for any child of Catie's. Now go pay."

Harper paid and shoved the receipt in his pocket. "You're not going to make me wrap this, are you?"

"Nope. We'll just take it as is. Let's get moving. We're late now. Where'd you park?"

"Behind the salon."

The drive to Catie's ranch house took over a half hour, but Harper didn't have to worry about making conversation. Amber chattered on about all kinds of things, some of which Harper found interesting, to his surprise. Amber wanted to learn barrel racing. Looking at her fake nails and platinum hair, he'd never have guessed racing would interest her. Though she had performed well enough on horseback to win first runner-up at the rodeo queen competition last summer. When Catie married and had to step down, Amber stepped up. She was now the reigning Bakersville rodeo queen. She had moved from Texas just a few months before last year's pageant, and she beat all the local girls except Catie. The McCray brothers had judged, and Harper knew how tough they were. Amber had earned the crown, no doubt.

"Do you ride much, Harper?"

"I run a ranch. I ride all the time."

"Do you compete?"

"I didn't last year. But I have in the past. I bust broncs and ride the occasional bull."

"Really? Bull riding? That's so dangerous."

"Not if you know what you're doing. I once saw Dusty McCray stay on a scary ass bull for six seconds. Course she gave herself a concussion afterward."

"Yes, I know. I heard about her and that bull of hers, El Diablo. They're still offering that half-mil purse, aren't they?"

"Every January at the stock show in Denver, and every summer at the rodeo here in town." He chuckled. "You're not thinking about taking up bull ridin', are you?"

"Heavens, no. I'll stick to horseback, thank you. I do admire a woman with those kinds of balls though, if you'll pardon the expression."

"Dusty McCray has balls and then some. That little girl's been through more than most."

"Yeah, Catie told me about her cancer, and about how she probably won't have any more children. I feel bad for her."

"It's a shame, no doubt. But she has quite a brood of nieces and nephews to dote on now, including Catie's Violet."

"She has a brother, doesn't she?"

"Yeah. Sam. He hasn't been around in a while. He lives up in Montana. They have a small ranch up there. I think he's planning to come for the rodeo in a few months though. He's a bronc buster like me."

"Hmm. Can you beat him?"

Harper let out a laugh. "He's damn good. But so am I."

Amber smiled, parting her cherry lips to reveal perfect white teeth. The skin around those gorgeous golden eyes crinkled. *Good God, the woman is hot.*

"I wouldn't mind learning bronc busting myself," she said, "though I think I'll stick to barrel racing for now. Maybe I'll ask Dusty McCray to teach me."

"She hasn't raced in years. Not since she had Sean."

"Yeah, true. I'm sure there's someone else around who can give me some pointers. Catie mentioned this guy who used to work for Chad a while back. He's back in town. His name's Blake something or other, and she says he knows the sport pretty well. He worked with his sister who's a champ."

Harper pursed his lips. He knew exactly who Amber was talking about. "Blake Buchanan, yeah." Blake Buchanan was also a champion coward and loser. He'd left town three years ago after impregnating the mayor's daughter. She'd had a miscarriage, but still. Course the man did know barrel racing.

"I was thinking I might check with him. I've heard he's a great coach."

Sweat beaded above Harper's lip. Why would he care if Amber worked with some loser who seduced an innocent young woman? Amber hardly looked innocent anyway. No one that hot could be innocent.

None of his business anyway.

Thank God. They arrived at Catie's, and the conversation

ended.

The place was already crowded as a stampede. Surely no one would have noticed if he hadn't shown up.

Nope. Catie would notice. He sucked in a breath, and with Amber clinging to his arm, walked inside.

"Amber!" Catie waded through the throng of people dragging a tall black-haired cowboy with her. "I'm so glad you're here. This is the man I've been telling you about. Blake Buchanan. This is Amber Cross, and you remember my brother, Harper."

Amber's golden eyes blazed as Blake approached.

On instinct, Harper wrapped his arm around Amber's waist and pulled her into his side. Warmth coursed through him.

"Hello there, darlin'," Blake said. "I hear you want to learn to race."

Harper's esophagus threatened to reverse. Here he stood, one arm around a stuffed horse, the other around a woman he wasn't interested in.

Was he?

Of course not. So totally not his type. But damned if he'd let her be bait for Blake Buchanan's snare.

"Where's my niece?" he said to Catie. Nothing like changing the subject.

"Chad's got her. They're out back. Come on out. Angie and Rafe arrived a while ago. We've got food and drink out there. It's such a gorgeous day. I'm so glad it's warm this spring."

Leave Amber here with this guy? No way. He handed the stuffed horse to Catie. "For Violet. Come on, Amber. Let's go get a drink."

"Oh. Okay." She touched Blake's arm. *Damn her.* "We'll

talk later, okay?"

"Sure enough. I'm gonna use the little boys' room and then I'll be right out with you."

Harper followed Amber out to the pool deck. The pool was covered. They'd fill it next month most likely. Late April was too early here in Colorado.

Everybody and his brother had shown up here. Caterers made their way through the crowds carrying platters of food. Several bars were set up. He led Amber to the closest.

"What'll you have?"

"Cosmo."

"Of course." What she saw in the froufrou drink was beyond him.

He ordered a beer for himself and looked around. Dallas and Annie McCray were here with their brood. Zach and Dusty and Sean. Joe Bradley, the mechanic. Doug Cartright, the sheriff. Judy had made it. His big sister, Angie, and her husband, Rafe Grayhawk, were talking to some people Harper didn't recognize. His mother and Uncle Jeff were making their rounds.

His father had been gone for over six months, but Harper still had a hard time accepting it. He owned Cha Cha Ranch now. He knew the ranching business. That part was no problem. But Uncle Jeff, Dad's brother, had surfaced after his death, claiming to own half of their western slope ranch, Bay Crossing. But that wasn't the biggest surprise. Turned out he was Angie's biological father. To top it all off, Mom had invited Uncle Jeff to live at the main ranch house at Cha Cha. So instead of moving in there, in the house he now owned, Harper stayed in his modest ranch house on the other side of the property. Not that he minded. He loved his house.

Harper had always known his parents had married because Mom had been pregnant with Angie. What he hadn't known was that Dad's younger brother, Jefferson Bay, had been in love with his mother. When Jeff went to prison for a crime he didn't commit, Mom had married Dad and convinced him the baby was his.

The thoughts choked in his throat. Harper still had a hard time with that one. He and Catie were Dad's kids, but not Angie. And his mother had tricked his father. Funny thing was, Angie was no longer holding a grudge. She had forgiven Mom and was working on a relationship with Uncle Jeff. If Angie wasn't upset, why should he be? After all, his father was still *his* father.

Course maybe Angie found it easier to accept because she was in love and newly married. She oozed happiness.

Harper had never been in love. He'd never understood what the fuss was about. He'd been interested in women, sure. Had dated quite a bit, a couple seriously, even. But fireworks had never gone off. He doubted that kind of love existed.

At least not for him. He had too much going on anyway. Heck, he had a ranch to run. His own ranch. He didn't need kids running around. If he wanted kids, he'd come see beautiful little Violet. And all the kids Angie and Rafe would have. They were already talking about starting a family. Course they lived at Bay Crossing on the western slope, but they'd come visit.

"Quit looking so sullen, Harper. Let's mingle." Amber grabbed his elbow and started toward Rafe and Angie.

"Hey, you two!"

Angie gathered them both in a hug. Amber's body crushed against his, and tingles shot up his spine. What the heck was going on?

"It's so good to see you guys."

"You just saw us at your wedding two weeks ago," Harper said dryly.

Angie swatted him on the arm. "What crawled up yours, Harp?"

"He's pissy because I made him come to this baby shower," Amber said. "He thinks showers are supposed to be for women."

"I think you're right," Rafe said.

"Yeah? Then why are you here?"

"Ang and I hadn't seen the baby yet till today. I wanted to see her."

Harper melted a little. "She's beautiful, isn't she?"

"Without a doubt." Rafe's black eyes softened as he looked at his wife. "I hope we have some good news soon."

"You're certainly putting a good amount of effort into it," Angie teased.

Harper tensed. He didn't need to think about his big sister having sex. Or his little sister for that matter. Though baby Violet was a wonderful result.

"Whose idea was this couples shower, anyway?" Rafe asked.

"Mine," Amber piped in. "It's really just an excuse for a big party, and Catie sure has the spread for it. Plus we all get to welcome Violet and pay our respects."

"It doesn't sound so bad when you put it that way," Rafe said with a chuckle. "I'm always up for a good party."

"Me too," Angie agreed. "Amber, we'll be here a few days. Can you get me in on Monday for a mani-pedi?"

"Absolutely." Amber took the last sip of her cosmo and looked up at Harper. "I see yours is nearly empty too. Can I get you another?"

"I'll get them." He took her glass, glad to be gone from the conversation. When his sister started talking mani-pedis, nothing interesting could possibly come of it.

★ ★ ★

Harper Bay was one fine-looking man. The second most eligible bachelor in Bakersville, behind mechanic Joe Bradley. At least that's what the local gossip columnist touted. Joe was handsome, no doubt, but Harper had a tousled sexiness—that mane of walnut hair that was always in disarray made Amber's heart patter. Judy talked all the time about how she'd love to get her fingers in it.

Amber'd love to get her fingers in it too. She eased away from Rafe and Angie and watched as Harper stood at the bar getting their drinks. She wasn't looking for a relationship. Nope, keep it simple—that was her motto. That's why she'd come to this small town, and she wasn't about to complicate her life with a man. Still, she couldn't ignore the sizzle that raced over her skin whenever Harper Bay was near.

"There you are, darlin'."

She turned to see Blake Buchanan. Also good-looking, but more refined with slicked back black hair and gentle brown eyes. A refined cowboy. That was a hoot.

"Hey, nice to see you again," she said.

"You know, I can't shake the notion that we've met before. Have we?"

Amber shook her head. "No. I'd definitely remember you. Besides, I've only lived here for a little over a year."

"Yeah? Where'd you move from?"

"San Antonio."

"Hmm. I spent some time there off and on. Is it possible we could have made each other's acquaintance at a party?"

"I wasn't the partying type." She didn't want to think about the life she'd left behind. Not when she'd found such a nice new one here in Bakersville. She was rodeo queen for goodness' sake.

He smiled. "I never forget a face. I'll definitely figure this out. We've met."

Amber's nerves skittered under her skin. What did he mean?

"So about your interest in barrel racing," he continued. "What are you looking for?"

Icy black fingers gripped the back of her neck. *Stay away,* her inner voice warned. *This guy will hurt you.* Her inner voice rarely surfaced, but when it did, she'd learned to trust it.

She cleared her throat. "I'll let you know on that. I haven't decided yet if I really want to get into racing."

"But Catie said you were chompin' at the bit."

Amber let out a nervous giggle. "She must have been exaggerating. Don't worry, I'll call you if I'm interested."

"How about a drink later, then? I'll take you to the Bullfrog."

She shook her head. "That's kind of you, but I'm already on a date today."

"With Catie's brother, I know. But I got the impression that was just a 'friends' thing."

"Not at all. It's a new relationship, but one I definitely want to explore."

God, I hope Harper can't hear any of this. He sauntered toward them holding her cosmo and another beer.

"Thank you, honey," she said, taking the drink from him.

His eyebrows arched. "You're welcome...sweetheart."

"Well, I can tell three's a crowd here," Blake said. "I'll see you all later." He walked away and then stopped dead in his tracks. He turned around and came back toward them.

"Miss Amber, I do believe I remember how I know you after all."

CHAPTER THREE

What in God's name was up with Blake Buchanan? And why in hell was he at Catie's party? Sure, he'd worked for Chad in the past, but he'd been gone three years. He'd left town amidst gossip, after disgracing Evie Luke, the mayor's daughter who was now the town librarian. Catie had still been in high school when he left. She hadn't known him at all. Why was she all of a sudden his champion?

A cold anvil landed in Harper's gut, and a truth settled in his mind. He must keep both Catie and Amber away from Blake Buchanan. The man was a jerk and up to no good. Harper felt it in the very marrow of his bones. It ached.

"Oh?" Amber fidgeted, her knuckles white as she grasped her martini glass.

"Yeah, back in San Antonio there's a place called Rachel's."

"Never heard of it," Amber said.

"Really? I'd swear I've seen you there. I'd never forget those legs."

"You're mistaken." She latched onto Harper's arm. "Let's go find Chad. I want to hold Violet."

Sounded good to Harper. Besides, he had a few questions for Miss Amber Cross himself. Every cowboy west of the Mississippi knew about Rachel's in San Antonio.

It was a strip club.

★ ★ ★

As she breathed in the fresh scent of baby powder, Amber's uterus skipped a beat. She silenced her reproductive organs and handed Violet back to Catie. "She sure is precious."

"Thank you." Catie beamed up at Chad. "We sure think so."

"Now you know I'll babysit anytime."

"Of course. Violet will love having her Auntie Amber come to sit. Won't you?" Catie cooed to the baby.

"I need to talk to you when you have a minute," Amber said.

"Oh, sure." Catie kissed the top of Violet's head. "She'll be ready to go down for a nap in about twenty minutes. I'll come find you."

"Perfect, thanks."

Chad handed the cosmo he'd been holding back to Amber, and he and Catie left to show Violet off to more people. Harper pulled Amber aside.

"Before you talk to Catie, you need to talk to me."

"What about?"

"About San Antonio."

Amber gulped.

"About Rachel's."

"What about it? I've never heard of it."

"You expect me to believe you lived in San Antonio and never heard of Rachel's? Sorry, not buyin' it."

Amber gulped again. She glanced down at her drink. Damn. Still half full. Couldn't use the old "could you get me another drink?" eye batting thing.

"Okay, okay. It's a gentlemen's club downtown."

"On the outskirts of town, and it's not a gentlemen's club. It's a strip club. And the strippers are known to take certain liberties. For money."

Amber's heart thudded. "Just how would you know all of this?"

"Easy." His lips curved into a sardonic smile. "I've been there."

"Oh?" She arched her eyebrows.

"Now don't go lookin' at me like that. Every cowboy goes to Rachel's at one time in his life. It's kind of a requirement I think. A rite of passage."

"And I suppose you paid for liberties?"

"Me? Hell no. I look but don't touch. I kind of feel sorry for those girls."

Amber tried to hide her surprise. "Sorry? Why? They make great money."

"So you *are* familiar with the place then."

Amber inhaled. Why wouldn't her insides stop quivering? Maybe she'd said too much. "Not really. I just know strippers usually make good money."

"Not all strippers. But at a place like Rachel's I'm sure the money can be great. Course it's been a long time since I've been there."

"Oh?"

"Yeah. Chad McCray—don't tell Catie—dragged me there when I turned twenty-one. He was twenty-three or twenty-four at the time. We were in San Antonio on an overnight for a rodeo."

"How old are you now?"

"Thirty."

Amber exhaled the breath she'd been holding. The flip-flops in her tummy slowed down a bit. He wouldn't recognize her.

"I can't believe you and Chad would go into that place."

"So you do know it."

"I've heard of it."

"Now I wonder...why in the world would Blake Buchanan think he had seen you there?"

"I'm sure I haven't the slightest idea." *God, how can I stop this conversation?*

"I'm thinking you're hiding something, Amber, and I aim to find out—"

Her drink fell out of her hand and hit the grass with a soft clump. She threw her arms around Harper's neck and smashed her lips to his.

Anything to shut him up. To end this conversation.

She hadn't expected the kiss to be so powerful.

Harper's lips were full, and oh, so soft. He parted them gently, and his tongue swept into her mouth, bitter and malty from his beer. Amber wasn't fond of beer, but on Harper it tasted like nectar. She let her tongue entwine with his. His response overwhelmed her. He wanted to kiss her. Heck, he was enjoying it.

So was she.

The kiss became more hurried, frantic. Their lips slid against each other's, searching and learning. Amber glided her fingers through Harper's tousled hair, soft as suede.

"Mmm."

His soft groan was more of a vibration against her lips than a sound. His arms tightened around her. One hand caressed the side of her neck. The other glided down her side, over the curve of her hips, and squeezed.

A delicate sigh left her throat, muffled by the kiss. His lips became her world. A soft, lush, romantic world, a world full of arousal and promise, a world where her nipples tightened, threatened to poke holes in her bra. A world where her sex heated. Lord, it had been a long time.

Had it ever been better?

She'd kissed a few men in her day. It had never been like this.

She jerked when a harsh sound cut into her dream.

Harper ripped his lips away from hers. Chad McCray stood next to them.

He cleared his throat again. That had been the harsh sound. A silly smile curved over his lips. "Hey there, Harp, Amber. Anything you all want to share with the rest of us?"

Harper's turn to clear his throat. "We were just—"

"Yeah, yeah. I see what you're doing. It's great, really. But this here's Catie's party for Violet. I don't want you two stealing her thunder."

"Oh, of course not." Amber's cheeks warmed. She was no doubt turning about thirty shades of scarlet. "We'd... I mean I'd...never do anything to spoil Catie's party."

"Me either," Harper said. "This was nothin', Chad. Just... we've had a little bit to drink and all..."

"Yeah." Blame it on the alcohol. That would work. No need to let everyone know she'd kissed him to make him forget about Rachel's. Evidently it had worked.

Now if she could only calm down the throbbing between her thighs.

Harper's lips were red and swollen. Were hers? She touched her fingers to them. They felt hot.

Catie ambled up, sans Violet. "Mary put the baby down

for a bit," she said to Chad, and then turned to Amber. "You wanted to talk to me?"

"Yeah, yeah I did. Would you two excuse us for a few?"

"Sure thing. Go on and have your girl talk," Chad said. "I'll take care of Harp. I have a few questions for him myself."

I'm sure you do. Sheesh. What would Harper tell Chad about their kiss? Did guys even talk about things like that? Hell if she knew. She really knew very little about men.

She and Catie wandered away from the crowd. Catie led her to a charming little bench behind the pool house. "So what's up?"

Amber plunked her behind down on the wooden bench. Where to start?

"What do you know about Blake Buchanan?" she asked.

"Not too much, really," Catie said. "He worked here for Chad a while back. Chad said he was a great worker. He knows tons about horses, I guess."

"Why'd he leave?"

"He left town because Evelyn Luke—you know, the librarian?—got pregnant. Blake was allegedly the father. At the time, Evie's dad was mayor of Bakersville. It's a small town. Pretty soon everybody knew."

"So what? Lots of women get pregnant out of wedlock. That's hardly a reason to chase a guy out of town."

"It is when the father of the girl tries to shoot the guy."

Amber perked up. "What?"

"Yeah. Mayor Luke went all crazy and ended up coming over here to Chad's, where Blake was living at the time, and holding him at gunpoint."

"What happened?"

"Well, he said Blake would marry his daughter or else.

Blake said no way, and I swear to God, Chad said he heard the gun cock."

Amber's muscles froze. One of her greatest fears was to be held at gunpoint. "Chad was there?"

"Yeah, they were in one of the stables."

"So did the guy shoot Blake?"

"Nope. Another guy walked in on them and ended up tackling Mayor Luke to the ground. I can't recall who it was. Chad could tell you. He's no longer here. Anyway, they called the sheriff and the mayor got carted off to jail."

"And Blake?"

"Left town running. Can't say I blame him. Evie ended up losing the baby. She still says it was Blake's. He denies it. So who knows? But I'm not going to persecute a guy for having sex. Heck, I got pregnant out of wedlock after sex with Chad, and I was a completely willing participant."

"Yeah, I know." Amber smiled. "That's what led to me being rodeo queen."

"And you're a much better one than I ever would have been."

Nausea gripped Amber's throat. If Catie only knew... Turns out she wasn't the perfect rodeo queen after all. She shook her head. She'd actually thought she could escape her past, start again somewhere new. A small town, where no one had heard of Rachel's. Where no one had ever heard of Ambrosia Love.

Why hadn't she dyed her hair? She'd thought to do it when she came to Bakersville. But she loved her ultra-light blond hair. It was natural, inherited from her Swedish mother. Judy could attest to its authenticity. She hadn't touched Amber's hair since she moved here.

Of course it wasn't her hair Blake had recognized. Nope,

damn those long legs. She couldn't change them, that was for sure. And truth be told, she didn't want to change them any more than she wanted to change her hair. They were part of her. She'd learned to like herself again. Why did Blake Buchanan have to come to town and threaten to spoil everything that was going right?

"Whatcha thinking?" Catie asked.

Amber shook her head again. "Just wondering, is all. You know, why Blake Buchanan would come back here after all the gossip."

"I hear he needs work. That's why I thought of him when you said you wanted to take up racing."

"Why doesn't Chad hire him at the ranch?"

"We don't really need anyone right now, and neither do Zach or Dallas. You know, I should ask Harper if he could use him at Cha Cha."

God, would this ever end? "I got the feeling Harper doesn't think too highly of him."

"Really?"

"Yeah." It wasn't actually a lie. Tension clearly existed between the two men.

"Well, I'll just have to have a talk with Harp then. Blake's a good guy who's had some tough breaks. He deserves a chance. I mean, look at my mama, giving my Uncle Jeff another chance."

"He's the father of her oldest child. There's a little bit of a difference there."

"I suppose. But still... Here comes Harp now."

The handsome cowboy ambled toward them, his lips pursed and forehead wrinkled.

Amber's tummy sank. He did not look happy.

CHAPTER FOUR

"Catie, why in the hell are you hanging out with Blake Buchanan?"

Amber exhaled, relieved. Harper was angry with Catie, not with her. Blake hadn't gotten to him, though Harper had no doubt already guessed her secret.

"He's a friend of Chad's."

"I just spoke with Chad. They aren't friends. Blake used to work here. Chad thinks he's okay, but they aren't friends."

"I just thought, since Amber wanted to learn to race and all, and Blake knows more about racing than anyone else in this town, except maybe Dusty—"

"You weren't thinking at all, little bit. The man's no good. I want both you and Amber to stay away from him."

Fine with me, Amber thought. Not that she took orders from men, not even a man with kissing skills like Harper Bay. This edict, however, she'd be happy to obey. In fact, if Harper decided to chase Mr. Buchanan right out of this town, she'd be okay with that.

"Chad says he's okay," Catie said.

"Chad says he was a good worker. That's what he told me. He also said he's not hiring him back right now, and he asked both his brothers not to either."

"Right. Because none of them need anyone."

"True enough. But also because Blake doesn't have the best reputation. He got chased out of Bakersville three years ago and he maintains his innocence. No one knows for sure who fathered Evie's miscarried baby except Evie herself. Hell, I don't care if it *was* Blake. They were both consenting adults at the time, and it's ancient history. So he runs off to San Antonio and now he's back. Why now?"

"I don't know," Catie said. "Maybe he missed it here."

"Could be." Harper stroked his chin. "But there's more to why Blake left San Antonio than you know."

"What might that be?" Amber asked. She couldn't help herself. Curiosity got the best of her.

"I can't tell you. I got the information in confidence from a friend."

"What friend?"

"Let's just say I made a quick phone call while Chad and I were talking."

"A phone call to whom?"

"I can't say. I'm sorry. Just stay away from Buchanan, both of you."

"Come on. You have to tell us," Catie said. "You must have told Chad."

"No, I didn't tell Chad, and I don't have to tell you. And I'm not going to. I will tell you that Blake no longer has contact with his parents, sister, and little brother. They wrote him off a couple years ago."

"So we're supposed to just do what you say because you say it? Without any information?" Catie whipped her hands to her hips.

Harper chuckled. "You look just like Angie when you do that."

"You're avoiding my question."

"That's right. I'm done talking about this." He turned to

Amber. "Another cosmo?"

Amber shook her head. "Nope. I always stop at two."

Catie let out a laugh. "Yup, she always stops at two. When are you going to tell me why that is, Amber?"

"I just know my limit, that's all."

"If you say so." Catie smiled and shook her head. "Since both of you are determined to keep secrets from me, I'm going to go check on Violet. You two try to stay out of trouble."

"She's got a belly full of fire worked up now," Harper said.

"Can you blame her?"

"I suppose not. You, on the other hand, didn't put up too much of a fight about Blake Buchanan."

Amber sighed. Did this man forget nothing? She might have to kiss him again. The thought pleased her. "Why should I? I hardly know him."

"That's not what he seems to think."

"Harper—"

"Look, I don't know why he thinks he knows you from Rachel's. And I don't give a damn if you used to take your clothes off for a living."

"I didn't—"

He put two fingers on her lips. A jolt shot through her.

"Let me finish. Please."

She nodded.

"I never thought you were my type at all, Amber. You're beautiful, no doubt, but different as all hell from the girls I'm used to. I hadn't given a thought to you in...that way. Until you kissed me, that is."

Amber's cheeks warmed. Was he attracted to her? What was he after? "I'm not sure what you're saying."

"I'm saying...aw, hell. I've never been any good at this. You want to go get a bite to eat after this shindig's over? Maybe talk a little?"

She smiled. "Harper Bay, are you asking me out?"

"I'm trying. You're not makin' it easy."

Amber's heart pounded. The kiss had been ecstasy for her. She hadn't thought it possible that he'd enjoyed it just as much. Yet she didn't want to complicate her life with a man right now. She was enjoying her alone time in this small town. Life was good.

Course Harper Bay just might make it better. Heck, it was only dinner, right?

She smiled. "I'd love to have dinner with you, Harper."

His lips curved upward in a smile that lit his whole face. He grabbed her hand, and electricity rushed up her forearm.

"I'm glad to hear that. How long do you think we have to stay at this shower you dragged me to?"

Amber laughed and entwined her fingers through his. "I guess we've stayed long enough."

★ ★ ★

Blake Buchanan drove back from Chad McCray's ranch to his hotel in downtown Bakersville. If he didn't find work soon, he'd be shit out of luck. He had debts that wouldn't wait much longer.

His cell phone vibrated in his pocket. His pal Bernie calling him back.

"Hey, Bern."

"Blake, sorry I missed your call. What's happening up north?"

"Same old same old. Lookin' for work. I need some help

with a situation."

"What can I do you fer?"

"Remember when we used to hang out at Rachel's?"

"Don't remind me. I still have the scars from my run in with that big ass bouncer."

Blake chuckled. Bernie sure knew how to get his ass in trouble. "You remember that sweet blond number with the legs?"

"Myrna?"

"No, blonder. She could wrap around a pole like nobody's business."

"Yeah, yeah. She left about a year or two ago, didn't she? What was her name? Andrea or something?"

Blake took a drink from the bottle of beer he held. "Ambrosia. She called herself Ambrosia Love."

"How could I forget? She was fine."

"She was. Still is." He lay down on his bed and set the beer on the night table. "You're not going to believe this, but she's right here in Bakersville, Colorado, working as a manicurist."

"No way."

"I'm not kidding. She's still hot as hell. Goes by Amber Cross."

"Wow. You gonna hook up with her?"

Blake's skin prickled. "I'd love it, but I have bigger fish to fry at the moment. Donetto isn't going to wait forever for me to pay him back. He already knows where I am."

"Well, of course he knows. You went back to a town you used to live in for God's sake."

"I came back here because I thought I could find work." He grabbed the beer and took another drink. "I was a damn good ranch hand at one time. I never should have gone to San

Antonio."

"Wrong. San Antonio was fine. You never should have gotten involved with Donetto. Period. I tried to warn you."

"I know, Bernie, I know. But listen, I need a favor."

"What's that?"

"I need the password to your brother's web site, the one that costs an arm and a leg?"

"I can't give you that."

"Look, I can't afford to pay the fee to log in myself. Please. I might be able to pay Donetto back if I can find the lovely Ambrosia on the site."

"Blake—"

"Please, Bernie. I'll owe you big."

Silence on the other end of the line. Blake's heart pounded.

Then, "Shit. All right. I guess it can't hurt. Log in as DickRobbins, password sw34789."

"Thanks, you're a pal."

"Just don't let Lance find out you're using his site for free. He'll fuckin' kill me."

"Understood."

They said goodbye and hung up.

Amber seemed like a nice enough girl, and Blake didn't want to hurt her, but better her than him at this point. She was tight with Catie Bay McCray, and that meant she had access to cash.

Blake needed cash.

He also needed his legs walking and his heart beating. If he didn't come up with cash soon, he'd lose all of that. Paul Donetto's goons would see to it.

He fired up his laptop. Damn thing was so freaking slow. Of course it was, it was five years old now. Rachel's in San

Antonio. Hardly the classiest place in town, but one of the biggest money-makers. He and his cronies had hung out there a lot. He fed in the URL to Lance's web site and started looking around.

Candy Hart. Eliza Bends. Taryn Apart. All ladies he recognized. He crept through page after page, discovering some new faces, enjoying some old ones.

Bingo.

Ambrosia Love.

Otherwise known as Amber Cross, best friend of Caitlyn McCray.

He didn't relish hurting such a beautiful young woman, but hey, times were tough. Surely young Amber would pay handsomely to keep the good folks of Bakersville from finding out about her past.

CHAPTER FIVE

"When you asked me to dinner, I figured you meant we'd go out." Amber smiled as Harper pulled his truck into the driveway of his ranch home on the Cha Cha Ranch grounds.

"Why? I love to cook. And I've got the best beef right here."

Amber let out a laugh. "Chad McCray always says he's got the best beef."

"He's dreamin'. He's got the third best. I raise the best here at Cha Cha, and a close second comes from Bay Crossing, our place on the western slope."

"Right, Angie's ranch."

"Angie's and Catie's, technically. But Catie lets Angie and Rafe run it. She's busy at Chad's ranch."

"Yeah, I know." Since when was her voice so wistful? "Catie sure is a lucky girl. She's got everything her heart desires."

"True that, especially since she's desired Chad McCray since she was five years old."

"I've heard the story." Amber grinned. "She stole Chad right out from under my nose when she got home from Europe last spring."

"Were you really interested in Chad McCray?"

Was that a twinge of jealousy in his voice? She wasn't sure. "No, not really. He's great looking and a lot of fun, but it was never more than a little fling. It didn't go anywhere anyway."

"You mean you didn't sleep with him?"

"Not that it's any of your business, but no, I didn't. I haven't slept with anyone since I moved here. I've hardly dated. It hasn't been a priority."

Oops. Had she said too much? She didn't want him to think she wasn't interested. She definitely *was* interested in him. Which surprised the heck out of her. He was a stud, for sure, but not really her type. A little too stiff. Why all the fuss about a co-ed shower? Sheesh. And too lawyerly. Course he was a lawyer, if only a non-practicing one. The real reason was she just wanted to be free of men for a while. Dancing naked in front of them for two years did that to a woman.

"Maybe we can change that."

"Are you saying you want to date me?"

His dark gaze seared her. "I think we're dating right now, aren't we?"

"I would have bet everything I had that I wasn't your type at all, cowboy."

"I didn't think you were either, but that kiss changed my mind."

Amber agreed. Her cheeks warmed. "It was something, that's for sure."

"So why did you kiss me anyway?"

"I think you already figured it out. I wanted you to stop talking about Rachel's."

"So...anything you want to tell me about that?"

"Not really."

"I won't judge you."

"I never said you would. It's a time in my life I prefer not to think about. A girl has to make a living, you know."

"True enough. And for what it's worth, I won't hold that

against you. Not that I'd want to see either of my sisters doing it."

"I wouldn't want to see either of your sisters doing it either. I care about them too much. It's not the noblest of callings. Little girls dream of being ballerinas or cowgirls or doctors or astronauts. I doubt any get a child-size pole and pretend to be a stripper."

Harper let out a laugh. "You're probably right."

"Geez, I sure hope so." *Change the subject, Amber.* "So what are you making me for dinner?"

"Like I said, I got the best beef right here, so...steak on the grill?"

"Sounds great."

"You're not one of those vegetarians?"

"Do I look like a vegetarian to you?"

He laughed. "Well, you're built great. But no, you look like a girl who likes a juicy steak."

"Yup. Rare. Better yet, blue."

"Blue? Seriously? I love 'em blue. Blue it is."

"What can I do to help?"

"Nothing."

"Come on. I love to cook."

"Okay," he laughed. "Grab some stuff out of the fridge and throw a salad together. And you can toss a few potatoes in the microwave. That ought to be a good dinner." He started toward the door and then turned. "And pick us out a bottle of wine from my rack."

"Cowboy, I know nothing about wine."

"Hmm. Okay, I'll pick the wine then." He ambled to his well-stocked rack and bent down.

Nice view. The man had one fine ass.

"Here's a nice Carmenére. You'll like it I think." He took it into the kitchen and Amber followed.

"Wow!" She couldn't help the awe in her voice. "This kitchen rocks. We could have some fun in here."

"I'm sure we could. And we could do some great cooking."

Amber giggled. "I meant cooking. Though this stainless steel surface looks extremely sanitary."

Harper opened the bottle of wine and poured two glasses. He handed one to Amber. "Let me know how it is."

She took a sip. "Like I said, I know nothing about wine, but this is good. Kind of spicy."

"There you go. Take another sip and let it float on your tongue for a minute and then ooze down your throat. Can you get the berries, the green pepper?"

"Green pepper?" She took a sip and followed his instructions. The wine was soft on her tongue. She swallowed. "I'll be damned. I do taste green pepper."

"Told you." He smiled. "I'm going to throw these steaks on the grill. Be back in a minute."

Instead of waiting, Amber followed him out to the patio and watched as he lit his gas grill.

He turned to her, his brown eyes blazing like the flames on the grill. "Amber?"

"Yes?"

"May I be frank?"

"I thought you were Harper." Bad joke. *Really, Amber? Did you really say that?*

He smiled that lopsided smile. "I'm serious."

"Okay, sorry. Sure. What?"

"Would you come to bed with me?"

"Huh?" Talk about spur of the moment. No talking? No

kissing? No heavy petting? No seduction attempt whatsoever?

"Here's the thing. I haven't been able to think straight since you kissed me at Catie's. All I can think about is you in my bed. I'm not sure I've ever wanted a woman this badly."

He advanced toward her. "You're so beautiful. And those lips...so full and red." He traced them with his fingers.

Her skin heated. Little jolts lit up where his skin touched hers. One finger trailed over her cheek, down her neck, and over the swell of her breast.

"I bet these are perfect like the rest of you."

Her nipple tightened.

His eyebrows arched. He'd noticed.

"I see you're not immune."

Immune? Who could be immune to him and his tousled charm? He was yummy. "Of course I'm not immune. Why do you think I agreed to have dinner with you? But I didn't agree to hop in the sack with you."

"No, you didn't. That's why I'm asking nicely."

"Have you ever seduced a woman, Harper? Because if you have, I hope you did a better job than you're doing right now."

He laughed. "I've had a few in my day. Though less than you probably think."

She smiled.

"I just don't see any reason to beat around the bush. I want you in my bed. I want to kiss those lips of yours until they're raw, I want to suck on those hard nipples until they're crimson from my whisker burn."

Amber heated. Her sex throbbed. How was he doing this?

"I bet you're sweet as a candy apple between your legs."

Harper Bay? How had she always thought he was some kind of Goody-Two-shoes? He was the second most eligible bachelor in Bakersville for a reason. She hadn't known he could talk so dirty. And she hadn't known it would make her crazy with desire.

"The steaks'll burn."

"We can save the steaks for later." He moved toward her so their bodies were touching. His hardness pressed into her belly.

Dear God. How could she want him so much? This was hardly her idea of a seduction, but if he pressed much harder she'd fall into his bed in a minute.

Yet he wasn't kissing her. He was simply gazing at her, with beautiful brown eyes so intent and so full of fire she thought they both might burst into flames at any moment. He traced the outline of her lips again, and she darted her tongue out and touched the tip of his finger.

He smiled. "You are so very sexy, Amber."

She let out a nervous giggle. "So are you."

Finally, he lowered his head and touched his lips to hers. Just a soft peck, barely a whisper. Passion shot to her core. From a little tiny kiss.

Seemingly of its own accord, her hand rose, cupped his cheek, his stubble prickly against her palm. She brushed his shoulder length hair back behind his ear. Soft as silk.

"Mmm, that feels nice." His voice was barely above a whisper.

"You have beautiful hair."

"So do you." He brushed his lips lightly against her cheek.

She shivered, her eyes closing. "It's natural, you know."

He stepped back. "Really?"

She opened her eyes. Why had she said that? "Yes, really. You didn't think it was?"

"I assumed it wasn't. It's still beautiful."

"Everyone thinks it's dyed. But it's natural. My mom was Swedish."

"Was? Is she gone?"

Amber's stomach knotted. "I...I don't know. I haven't seen her since I was sixteen."

"Oh?"

"She kicked me out of the house."

Harper grabbed her hand. "I had no idea. What happened?"

"It's a long story."

He led her to the living room. "Let's sit down."

"Okay."

"You want to tell me?"

"It's no big deal. I stayed with a friend and went to the vocational high school. That's where I learned to do nails. I got my license and my high school diploma. With honors even. But I had to leave my friend's house once I was out of school. Her mother kicked us both out. I had a hard time finding a job right out of beauty school, and long story short, she and I ended up at Rachel's when we were barely eighteen."

"Wow."

"I couldn't serve alcohol. Couldn't *drink* alcohol. Not legally anyway. But I could take my clothes off. Something doesn't seem right about that."

"I agree."

She sighed. "It was a living. A pretty good one, truth be told. I made enough to take some riding lessons. I had done a little when I was younger and my mother kept house for a rancher. I was pretty good too."

"I know you were. You are, I mean. I saw you ride at the

rodeo queen competition, remember?"

She smiled. "That's right. Judy let me use her horse. She was a beauty. But anyway, the money was good. I can't lie."

"Yes, I'm sure it was."

She shifted her shoulders, hoping he'd believe what she was going to say. "But I swear, Harper, I never did any of that other stuff. I only stripped."

"I believe you." He took her hand and caressed her palm. "What happened with your mom? Why did she kick you out?"

"She was a drunk. She couldn't afford both me and her booze. The booze won."

"And your father?"

"Never knew him. He's supposedly a bronc buster named Morgan Cross. His name's on my birth certificate, but I've never met him. He wasn't part of my life. I'm not sure my mother ever told him about me. In fact, I've wondered on more than one occasion if she just made the name up."

Harper's eyes widened. "I don't think she made up that name."

"Why do you say that?" A warm ray of hope shot through her veins. "Do you know him? I never could find anything on the net about him."

"Not by that name, you wouldn't. But I assure you he does exist. He goes by the name Thunder Morgan. He retired a few years ago."

"Well, he must have brown eyes then. My mother's are ice blue. She's got the typical Scandinavian coloring. So do I, except for these darn eyes."

"I think he has brown eyes, but I never really paid much attention. His hair's a sandy blond. He and my father were friends. He'd come by the ranch every so often, usually during the rodeo. He hasn't been around for a few years, but he showed up at my father's memorial service."

"*I* was at your father's service!"

"I know. Freaky, huh? He was only at the church though. He didn't come back to the house. He's a good man, Amber. I doubt he knew he had a daughter. If he had, he would have been a part of your life."

"Is he married?"

"Nope. Never married that I know of. He was on the rodeo circuit forever. Not much of a life for a family."

"A better life than living with a drunk, I'd bet."

"Yeah, maybe. Hey, that's why you never drink more than two drinks, isn't it?"

"Yeah, pretty much. I've had a few bad experiences with alcohol, so now I keep to my limit. I figure alcoholism is in my genes. I'm not giving it any help."

He smiled and twirled one finger through a lock of her hair. "That's smart."

"Even when I was at Rachel's, I never did the booze or drugs like the other girls did."

"You're very strong."

She squirmed, embarrassed by his near reverence. She was so not worthy of it. "Don't put any halos on me. It's not like I never got drunk before. I did. Twice to be exact. The first time I blacked out and lost several hours. Scared the hell out of me. You'd think it would have scared me enough never to do it again, but I was young and stupid."

"We all are, baby. There's not a one of us who doesn't do something stupid when we're eighteen."

She smiled. What a nice guy he was. "The second time I ended up in bed with a stranger. Thank goodness he turned out to be a nice guy. That's when I got scared straight and decided not to tempt fate. No more than two drinks at a time. Like I said, alcoholism is probably in my genes."

"I still say you're strong."

"Not strong enough. If I were, I'd never have ended up at Rachel's."

Tears filmed over her eyes. Why in hell was she talking to Harper Bay about this stuff? And how did he know her father? Crazy. Just crazy.

"I'm sure you did the best you could. Stripping may not be the classiest job out there, but it's an honest living. As long as there are men in the world, there will be a market for beautiful women to take their clothes off."

"You're not extolling the virtues of your gender, cowboy."

"Baby, men are rarely virtuous. We all think with our dicks half the time."

Amber couldn't help but laugh. "You got that right."

"You have a beautiful smile, baby, and a great laugh." He wiped a stray tear from her cheek. "Let's get those steaks ready."

Amber shook her head. "The steaks can wait. I want to take you up on your previous offer. I'd like to go to bed."

CHAPTER SIX

A crackle of energy passed through the air—hot, raw, and carnal. Amber's skin sizzled. Did Harper feel it too? A deep sexual hunger stirred to life in her gut.

Harper turned out to be a gentle lover. He removed her clothes with care, slowly and deliberately, to the point where she wished he'd hurry up a little. The spiral of need burst out of her belly and flowed like molten honey through her veins. Her arousal—unlike anything she'd ever known—sent sparks over her whole body.

Every touch tingled as though she were holding a blow torch. She looked down at his crotch, at the arousal apparent beneath his jeans. She gulped and dragged her gaze back up to his face. His dark eyes consumed her with raw need. Sensations of ice and fire raced up her spine. Her hunger for him gnawed at her, and the tickle between her legs intensified.

He'd discarded her shirt already, and he stroked up her ribs, to the edge of her bra. She leaned toward him, as though a magnet drew her. His finger reached underneath her bra and stroked the sensitive skin of her breast.

Her breath caught. Her nipples tightened against the satin of her bra. Slowly, slowly he caressed, until the need to shout at him to take the damn bra off almost overwhelmed her.

As though he read her mind, he deftly unhooked the offending garment and tossed it to the floor. Her ample breasts fell gently against her chest. The air hit her nipples and they tightened even further. He leaned down, and his firm wet mouth closed over one peak.

Such sweet suction, such gentleness. He drew on the nipple, sucking, tonguing, teasing. The ache between her legs heightened. With his other hand he cupped her other breast, and she leaned into him, letting his palm rub against her, hold her. Fingers clamped around the nipple and she sucked in a breath. Just a touch of pain, the right amount. It spiraled downward and intensified her need.

"Mmm. Beautiful." His breath caressed her skin. "Gorgeous breasts, baby."

Thank you, she said in her mind. It came out as a soft sigh, the air blowing wisps of his silky hair into further disarray.

His other hand wandered to her crotch. Through her jeans, he rubbed her most intimate place. "Are you getting wet, baby? Wet for me?"

Another sigh was her answer.

"I'm hard for you, Amber. So hard. God, I want you."

Amber wasn't sure she'd ever wanted a man this much, this intensely. How could this be happening? With Harper Bay? Brother to her best friend? They didn't have chemistry did they? Couldn't possibly.

Yet her body responded to his touch like it had to no other man's. Not that she was overly experienced. In fact, she hadn't ever had a serious relationship. A couple dates here and there, two one-night stands, one of which had been a drunken mistake. What did it feel like to have real chemistry? To fall in love?

She foisted the thought from her mind. This was not love. Harper certainly wasn't in love with her. So he knew a few things about her past now and he didn't hold them against her.

That didn't mean he was in love with her. To the contrary, it only meant he was a nice guy.

Was it too soon to fall in bed with him?

Yeah, it really was. She pulled away.

"Baby? You all right?"

"Yeah, yeah. I'm fine. I'm just not sure this is the right thing to do after all."

"Oh?"

"I mean, we hardly know each other."

He pushed a stray curl behind her ear. "I know I'm attracted to you. I know I'm hard for you. I want you. And I know you want me. If I reached into your panties right now I'd find you wet. I can tell by looking at you. Your cheeks are ruddy, your eyes smoky, your lips swollen and trembling. You want this, Amber."

She couldn't deny it. "It's not a question of what I want. It's a question of what is right."

"We're attracted to each other. We want each other. What's not right about that?"

How could she tell him when she didn't know herself? All she knew was that Harper was someone special. Someone she could actually imagine a future with. And she didn't have time for a man right now.

Well, that wasn't exactly true. She'd just decided against men for the time being. She wanted to finally be her own person and not be subject to the whims of men like she'd been during those years at Rachel's.

But Harper? Yes, Harper was a decent guy. A guy she could fall for. So the last thing she wanted was a one-night stand with him. If she slept with him now, she'd destroy any chance for a relationship.

Was he even looking for a relationship? Probably not. Still, sleeping with him now felt both very right and very wrong.

Very right because she was wet and horny and extremely attracted to him.

Very wrong because he was the type of guy she wanted in her future, and she might destroy that possibility if she fell into bed with him on the first date.

"I'm sorry. I know I said I wanted this." She scooted away from him. Had to be away from him to get her body under control. Still she shuddered. It wasn't working. "I was feeling close to you. I told you things I haven't told anyone, and I'm not really sure why. But I don't sleep around. I don't want you to get the wrong idea about me."

He cocked his head. "You worked at Rachel's."

A sword of anger lanced through her. How dare he assume— "As a dancer, damn it. Not as a prostitute!"

"You're right. I'm sorry. I don't know why I said that." He stood. "I'm a big boy. It's been a long time since I've slept with anyone, and the truth is, I'm horny as hell for you. But I'm also a gentleman. I understand a lady can change her mind."

"Thank you." She smiled, and her anxiety eased a bit. "I assure you I'm not in the habit of being a tease. If you want me to go, I will. We don't need to have dinner."

His dark eyes danced as he grinned. "Of course we do. I've got the steaks all ready to go. I hope you'll stay."

Thank God he wasn't angry. "I'd love to stay. Thank you."

"But if you expect me to have dinner with you and not jump your bones right here and now, you have to do something for me."

"Of course. What's that?"

An adorable dimple cut into his left cheek. "Put your shirt

back on, baby. Right now you look good enough to eat."

Amber warmed as she donned her bra and shirt. "Better?"

"Not really," he teased, "but it'll do for now. There's one thing we need to get clear though."

"Yeah? What's that?"

"I like you, Miss Amber, and I'm not done tryin' to get you into my bed."

She laughed. "That's fine by me. If we continue to go out and we like each other, that's where we'll end up. I'm looking forward to it."

His dark eyes gleamed. "So am I." He stood. "Now about those steaks."

"I'll get our salad ready."

She went to the kitchen to start work as Harper went outside to the patio to put the steaks on the grill. He came back in with a serious look on his face.

"One thing I want to know."

"Sure. What?"

"How did no one know till now that Thunder Morgan is your dad?"

"I never told anyone his name till you." She shook her head. "Funny. I told you a lot of things tonight that I never talk about. My mother, for example. Rachel's. I've never told Catie or Angie any of that stuff."

"Still, you knew his name."

"You got a cutting board?" Amber rinsed off a tomato. "I knew it was Morgan Cross, not Thunder Morgan."

Harper grabbed the board out of a cupboard and handed it to her. "True. I guess most people wouldn't know his real name. I only know it because he was friends with my dad."

"Can you tell me a little about him?" She sliced into the

tomato's red flesh.

"Careful, I've nearly de-fingered myself with that knife." He winked. "He's a good guy. Retired now."

"How old is he?"

"I haven't a clue. Probably in his late fifties or early sixties. He knew my dad from his days on the western slope. He worked as a ranch hand for my great-grandpa when he was just starting out. Once he took a few good-size rodeo purses, he left the ranch and went out on the circuit. Never married, never had kids. Or rather, I never knew he had kids. My guess is he doesn't know either."

"I seriously thought my mother made up the name to put on the birth certificate." She dumped the tomato into the salad bowl and began chopping a few scallions.

"He's a real person, and she told you he was a bronc buster, right?"

"Yeah. They must have met when he was in Texas doing a rodeo or something. She never told me more than his name and the fact he busted broncs. I stopped asking after a while. Then she kicked me out."

"Why? Why did she kick you out?"

Amber sighed and tossed some bagged lettuce into the bowl. "Who knows? She was a drunk, Harper. I have no clue why she did half the things she did. I wasn't much of an expense to her. I did all the cooking and cleaning. If I didn't the place was a sty."

"Did she work?"

"At the post office, yeah."

"At least she held down a job."

"As far as I know. Once I left I never looked back. I have no idea what she's doing now."

"You mean you haven't seen her?"

"Heck no." Amber tossed the salad to keep her hands busy while past emotion crept into her. She held it at bay. "Why would I want to see the woman who kicked me out of her house when I was only sixteen? If it weren't for my friend Laura taking me in, I'd have been on the streets."

"I guess I can't blame you." Harper's arms slipped around her waist from the back. "I'm sorry life was so tough for you. It's hard to imagine a mother not wanting her child. My mother loves her children so much."

"You don't know how lucky you are."

"I was mad as hell when I found out she'd duped my dad about Angie's paternity. It wasn't fair to him or to Jeff, my uncle."

"Angie's real father, yeah I know." Amber leaned back into Harper's hard chest. Instantly her agitation lessened. Ahhh. What a remedy for the anxiety produced by the subject of her mother.

"But I'm beginning to understand why she did it." Harper's breath was warm against her scalp. "She did it for Angie. To give her a good life. She married a man she didn't love so her child would have a great life. There's a lot of selflessness in that."

"There's a ton of selflessness in that, Harper. Don't hold a grudge forever."

"You should take your own advice, baby." He turned her around to face him. "Do you ever think about seeing your mother? Working things out?"

Her tummy churned. Here came the agitation again. "There's a huge difference. My mother never did anything out of selflessness. Who in hell kicks out a sixteen-year-old girl?

That's plain selfish."

"True enough." Harper trailed one finger over her outer ear. "Maybe she had her reasons though."

"Yeah. She couldn't afford me plus the booze. Typical Karen Hedstrom priorities."

"That's her name? Karen Hedstrom?"

"Yup."

"And you never knew your father at all?"

"Nope. She never saw him again after that night."

Harper's brow furrowed. "Interesting."

"Why?"

"Why she'd put his name on your birth certificate. Give you his last name."

Amber shrugged. "Doesn't seem so weird to me."

"Maybe not. You're twenty-two right?"

"That's right."

"Twenty-two years ago Thunder Morgan was already pretty well-known. If you are truly his daughter, why wouldn't your mother have tried to contact him to get child support?"

"Don't ask me. I have no idea how Karen's mind works. She was probably too inebriated to think of it."

"Hmm. Doesn't seem to make sense."

"It's too late now. I'm way too old to get child support. He wasn't there when it counted."

Amber tried to turn around and grab the salad bowl, but Harper stopped her. "If you'd known your father was famous, would you have tried to contact him?"

"I don't know." She shook her head. "Why the third degree, Harper? Maybe he's not even my father. I really don't care. I've made it on my own for the last six years. I don't plan to start taking help from anyone now."

"I'm not saying you need his help. But wouldn't you like to know him?"

"What good would it do now? He didn't want me before."

"Baby, that's not fair." His strong hands gripped her shoulders. "He didn't *know* about you before."

She sighed. "Look. You now know more about me than pretty much anyone in the world. Could we just eat our steaks?"

"Crap, the steaks!"

He ran outside. A few minutes later he returned. "Well, they won't be blue, but they'll be medium rare. That okay with you?"

She laughed. "That's just fine. I'll put the salad on the table. And when we sit down to eat, could we please talk about something besides my genetic makeup?"

"Absolutely." He brushed his lips over hers.

CHAPTER SEVEN

Harper had a perpetual hard on thanks to Amber Cross. And he had a sneaking suspicion that she *was* his type after all. He'd have loved to screw her brains out the previous evening. In fact, he'd brought it up because he'd assumed she'd hop in the sack with him. She'd worked as a stripper, right? Course that didn't mean she was easy, and he berated himself for being so prejudiced. Even so, she'd almost gone through with it. When she changed her mind he thought he'd explode. But now, having had the night to ponder it, he was glad they hadn't done the deed.

Amber Cross was special. Maybe even the one. He'd never in a million years imagined it would be her. But clearly they had chemistry, both physical and emotional.

She wasn't a quick fuck.

The girl'd had one hard life. For the life of him, he couldn't figure out why her mother wouldn't have gone after Thunder Morgan for child support. Unless Thunder Morgan wasn't Amber's father after all. But then why would Karen have named him on her birth certificate?

Amber was holding something back. Harper wasn't sure what it was, but he was sure of one thing.

He was going to find out.

★ ★ ★

Amber had Sunday off. She relaxed in her studio apartment above the beauty salon. It was tiny but cheap, and it worked for her. She had finally saved up enough money to buy a tablet, and she fired it up after she'd downed her first cup of coffee.

Her Google search? None other than sweet Daddy himself, Thunder Morgan.

He had his own web site, of course.

Her heart nearly stopped. There on the web page were her light brown eyes.

She'd always been a dead ringer for Karen Hedstrom, except for the eyes.

He was handsome—sandy gold hair graying at the temples. An older man now, but she flipped through his gallery and caught sight of him in his younger years. Wow. Buff and beefy, just the way Karen liked her men.

Why on earth would he have been interested in bedding a worn-out drunk like her mother?

And why, why, *why* hadn't her mother gone after him for child support?

Harper was right. Something was up with this story. Amber scanned each page of the web site. Nowhere was the name Morgan Cross mentioned. She did a Google search cross referencing the two names. Nothing.

Either Thunder Morgan was not Morgan Cross, or he had left that name behind for some reason.

Two things niggled at her.

First, Harper would not lie. He was Catie's brother, and he was a good man. He wasn't a liar. If he knew Morgan Cross was the birth name of bronc buster Thunder Morgan, that was how it was.

Second. She couldn't overlook it or deny it. The man stared at her from her computer screen with her own eyes.

"I'll be damned," she said aloud.

She had questions. Tons of questions. She should go to Karen. But she hadn't spoken to the woman since she'd been kicked out of her house. What would she do? Go to San Antonio and show up on her doorstep?

Hi, I'm the daughter you threw out with the trash. Uh, how come you neglected to tell me my father was Thunder Morgan? And how come you neglected to tell him he had a kid?

She couldn't do any of those things. She didn't have two nickels to rub together. How would she get to San Antonio? On her looks? Hardly.

Her cell phone interrupted her thoughts.

She smiled. It was Harper. They'd exchanged numbers last night.

"Good morning, beautiful," he said. "Feel like some coffee?"

"I'm on my second cup already." She laughed.

"How about I come get you and we'll head to Rena's for some more. And maybe a croissant or two?"

"A croissant? You mean a cowboy like you doesn't want a hearty bacon and egg breakfast?"

His chuckle warmed her ears. "Well, that does sound good."

"Come on over to my place then. I'll make you breakfast. And my coffee's better than Rena's."

"Better than Rena's? Them's fightin' words."

"She brews a good pot, for sure. But mine's better. Strong, thick, and black, like my men."

"Huh?"

She giggled into the phone. "Just a joke, cowboy. From a movie I saw once."

"I won't turn that down. I'll be over in half an hour or so."

She took a quick shower and let her hair hang in wet waves around her face and shoulders. Then she tidied up the place, which didn't take long given its size, and started a fresh pot of coffee. She looked in her small fridge. Plenty of eggs and bacon, good. Also a few apples and a few cartons of yogurt. That was about it. Time to do some shopping. She'd get to that later today.

She started the bacon, and by the time a knock sounded on her door, the tiny place was alive with the aroma of smoky pork.

"Come in," she called.

"Hi there." Harper entered carrying a bouquet of wild flowers. He handed them to her.

"Thank you. That's so sweet." She grabbed a jar out of a cupboard and put the flowers in water.

"I've never been up here before," he said.

"It's small but comfy. It's actually really convenient to have everything in one room."

He sat down on the edge of the bed. "A double, huh? Not a lot of room."

"Don't need a lot of room just for me." She gave him what she hoped was a teasing smile and served up a plate of bacon and eggs. "Here you go."

"Smells great."

"Just sit down at my little table there." She pointed. "Dig in."

"You've fixed this little place up real nice."

"It worked well since this is about all I had to bring with me. I roomed with my friend Laura and another girl in San Antonio. Most of the furniture belonged to the other girl. I was thrilled when Judy showed me this place. I knew I wouldn't have to go out and buy a lot of stuff I couldn't afford."

"Makes sense." He took a bite of eggs. "Mmm. Good. So, I've been thinking."

"About what?"

"About your situation."

She gulped down a sip of coffee, her nerves on edge. Was he going to bring up Rachel's again? "What situation might that be?"

"About your dad, Thunder Morgan."

Oh, that was all. She breathed easier. "Funny you should mention him. I was just doing some research this morning."

"And?"

"And he was already a pretty big name by the time he hooked up with my mother. So I'm confused why she didn't tell him about me."

"Maybe she didn't know how to get in touch with him. The world wide web wasn't as worldwide twenty-two years ago."

"That's true, but he was a pretty big name, especially in rodeo country."

Harper swallowed his mouthful. "Well, there's one way to find all this out."

"And that is?"

"You could ask her."

Amber nodded. She'd thought of that, but... "Yeah, I suppose. But I literally haven't seen her or spoken to her since she kicked me out."

"So?"

Clearly Harper wasn't getting it. Of course not. He'd had a model childhood. "It's a little awkward."

"She's your mother, and you deserve some answers."

"I deserve a lot of answers. Doesn't mean I'm going to get any."

"Can't hurt to try."

She sighed and pushed her plate to the side. "The thing is, Harper, it *can* hurt. I don't want to go back to San Antonio. I left for a reason. I got the hell out of Rachel's. I don't want to go back there."

"Even to find out more about who you are?"

"Can't I find out from here? I mean, you said you know Thunder Morgan. You could contact him."

"Yes, I could do that, I suppose."

"Would you?"

"For you?" He leaned forward—the table was so small—and brushed his lips against hers. "Anything."

Her skin erupted in tiny bumps. Just a small peck, and here she was ready to hop into the sack with him again. And with her bed only twenty feet away—in plain view, still rumpled—it'd be darn easy.

Nope. Not going there. Not tumbling into bed with Harper just because he was tousled and sexy and oh so sweet to her.

She stood. "More coffee?"

He shook his head. "I'm doing fine. What are you doing the rest of the day?"

"No plans. I need to hit the grocery store. Pretty much all I had left was eggs and bacon. You got lucky this morning."

"Not as lucky as I'd like to." His voice was soft, husky, so very masculine.

She swooned just a little bit.

"I've been thinkin'," he said, his voice huskier than seconds before.

"About what?"

"About us."

"There's an us?"

"There could be, I think. I'm not lookin' for anything serious. Not just yet, anyway."

"Neither am I," she said and meant it, but her heart sank just a little.

"But I know one thing. I really want to kiss you right now."

He stood and took the coffee pot from her hands. Amber's breath caught as his finger trailed over her lower lip.

"You have such a gorgeous red mouth, baby." He cupped both of her cheeks and touched his lips to hers. The kiss was light and teasing, just enough to still her resistance.

Not that she had any resistance. What a crock.

He tasted of the robust coffee, the smoky bacon, with just a hint of minty outdoorsiness, an unexpected taste of wildness. He brushed his firm full sexy lips back and forth over hers.

Her eyelids fluttered closed, and she gave herself to the kiss, to the passion and desire that flowed between them. How difficult it would be not to fall in bed with this man! The moist heat of his mouth against hers tormented her, made her want more. Made her want all of him.

The kiss became stronger, more possessive, every bit as raw and unapologetic as it was tender and sweet.

Perfect.

The perfect kiss.

She sighed into his mouth, let her tongue entwine with his. She thrust her hands into his silky hair, let it flow through her fingers. So soft, like silk fringe—and beautiful, tousled, and sexy like the rest of him.

His groan vibrated against her lips and gums. The pressure of his lips increased, and he kissed her as though he wanted to devour her right then and there.

Without thinking, she stepped backward, backward, until the back of her legs hit the side of her bed. She sat, pulling him with her, until they were lying, him on top, still kissing with the frantic desire of new lovers.

His lips left her mouth and crept over her cheek to her ear. "I want to give you pleasure, Amber. I want to show you how good I can make you feel."

Yes, yes, yes, she said in her mind. Her sex pulsed between her legs. Her nipples tightened into buds so hard she was sure they'd freeze and fall off. They ached for his lips, his teeth, his tongue. She wanted to rip off her clothes and climb on top of him.

His strong hands roamed over her shoulders, across the swell of her breasts still covered by clothing. Fingers fumbled at the waistband of her jeans, and soon he was tugging them over her hips.

"Is this okay?" he whispered.

She nodded.

"Naughty girl. No panties."

She let out a soft laugh. "I was in a hurry."

He tossed her jeans on the floor. She lay, her body taut and full of tension, tight as a bowstring, her breasts and shoulders still covered, but naked from the waist down.

He touched her clit, and she nearly shattered right there. He rubbed her softly, moved downward into her folds.

"Mmm. So wet for me, baby."

Her body thrummed to the point she was sure he could

hear the low purr. She thrashed her head from side to side on her rumpled comforter.

His fingers picked up speed, just a little, and he eased one inside of her while his thumb circled her clit.

She sighed.

"You like that, baby? Do I make you feel good?"

She closed her eyes, basked in the warmth covering her body, the desire flowing through her veins. "Yes, yes. Just like that, Harper."

"Mmm. You're beautiful. I need to taste you."

When his lips replaced his thumb on her clit, she soared to the ceiling. It had been a long time since anyone had made her feel this good. She wasn't sure anyone ever had, truth be told.

Sensation after sensation bombarded her body.

"God, baby, you're so sweet," he said against her folds, his breath a soft caress.

He continued to stroke the inside of her with his finger, and he added another as his tongue worked the rest of her flesh. She tangled her fingers in his hair, moving her hips against him, guiding his mouth in the right rhythm.

The spasms started in her clit, rocked through her wet channel, and spread up into her torso and then outward to her arms and legs until even her toes tingled. She flew, she danced, she soared, all without leaving the bed.

"That's right, baby, come for me." Harper thrust his fingers in and out of her in a racing rhythm matching her breaths.

"God, oh God," she heard herself scream. "Good. So good!"

When she finally floated downward, encased in pure nirvana, she opened her eyes. His head was still between her legs, his lips and chin glistening with her cream. She couldn't speak. Could barely move her head.

He smiled, his brown eyes glowing. "Again," he said, and he went back to work.

CHAPTER EIGHT

Going down on Amber was pure pleasure. Though he loved pleasing a woman, Harper had never enjoyed this part of sex more than he did at this moment. She tasted of citrus and honey and warm musky woman. Her beautiful pink flesh tantalized him. He couldn't get enough of her. His dick pulsed inside his jeans.

He aimed to keep it there. She didn't want to rush into anything, and truthfully, neither did he. This was for her. Just about her.

It might kill him, but so be it.

He brought her to a second orgasm, and then to a third. He started going for a fourth, but she begged him to stop.

"Please, Harper. You're going to kill me."

He grinned at her. "But what a way to go."

She fisted her hands in his hair and pulled him toward her. Their mouths mashed together, and he let her taste herself on his tongue. Mmm, did she enjoy that flavor as much as he did? From the moans and sighs coming from her, she did.

They kissed with passion, with fire, with unbridled lust. He ground his erection against her firm supple thigh. God, those legs. Wrapped around and over his shoulders they'd been heaven.

A vision popped into his head, of Amber's amazing legs wrapped around a silver pole at a strip club. At Rachel's.

He broke the kiss.

Why'd he have to think of that? Yes, he'd once thought she had the body of a stripper...

She looked up at him, her golden eyes wide. "Is something wrong?"

He shook his head. Nothing was wrong. He just didn't like thinking of her that way. He didn't judge her. At least he didn't think he did. She hadn't had much choice after her mother kicked her out. At least she'd finished school first.

"No. I'm fine."

She smiled. Oh, she could kill a man with that knockout smile.

"Good. Now I think it's your turn."

He shook his head. "Nuh-uh. That was for you, baby. Only for you."

"Surely you don't expect me to be so selfish."

"I certainly do." He cracked his wiseass grin. "And don't call me Shirley."

She burst into laughter. "The same movie! I love those corny lines."

"Me too," he said, laughing.

He got up. Still hard as a rock.

Oh well. It was Sunday. Ranches didn't stop on Sunday. "I have to get going. A million things to do at home."

"Are you sure you don't want—"

He shushed her with two fingers on her beautiful swollen lips. "I wanted to please you. And I want you to know I'm not just in this for sex. I like you."

"Wow."

"And just so you don't think my actions were completely altruistic"—he kissed the top of her forehead—"I enjoyed the hell out of that."

"That makes two of us." She stood. "I *will* pay you back though."

He kissed her rosy cheek. "I certainly hope so. But on your own time. When you're ready."

"What if I'm ready right now?"

Good God! He wasn't made of stone. "Baby, I'm tryin' to make a point here."

"That you're a gentleman. I know."

"That I want you, but that I'm willing to wait."

"What if I'm not?"

He pressed his lips to her forehead. "Good. The sooner the better in my book. But not today. I've gotta run. I'll call you later, okay?"

Her smile turned into a little pout. Man, even frowning she was beautiful. "Okay," she said.

"Thanks for breakfast."

"You're very welcome. Anytime."

"I'm counting on it." He gave her big wet kiss.

The weakening in his knees surprised him. This woman had a huge effect on him. And he liked it. He liked it very much.

He grabbed his Stetson, winked, and left.

★ ★ ★

Amber was arranging groceries in her tiny fridge after a quick trip to the store when a knock on the door interrupted her thoughts.

Harper! Her heart did a flip-flop. He'd come back. She couldn't wait to see him. They'd make love now. She wouldn't make him wait any longer. She opened the door with a huge smile on her face.

That turned into shock. And a little bit of horror.

Blake Buchanan. Blake Buchanan holding a laptop.

"Hello, Amber."

"Mr. Buchanan. What can I do for you?"

"Now that's a right good question. May I come in?"

"What for?"

"I have something I want to show you, and after that, I think you'll agree we have tons to talk about."

She gripped the doorknob with her sweaty palm. "If you want to talk, call me on the phone."

"Then I wouldn't be able to show you what I want to show you."

"I'm sure I could not care less."

"I think you're wrong about that...Ms. Love."

Amber's stomach churned. Ms. Love. Ambrosia Love. He did remember her.

Play dumb. He can't have anything. You didn't do anything wrong.

She cocked her head. "Excuse me?"

His brown eyes shot darts. Had she really thought them gentle when she first met him?

"Ms. Love. Ambrosia Love. That was your stage name at Rachel's, wasn't it?"

She loosened her grip on the doorknob, tried to relax. "I can't see what business that is of yours."

"I think you might disagree once you see what I have to show you. May I come in?"

"No."

"Well then, I'll have to send this stuff over the Internet, and security being what it is these days, I can't be held responsible for who might see this information."

She swallowed and hoped he didn't notice. "What information do you think you have, Mr. Buchanan?"

"Information that I don't think you'd want anyone in the good town of Bakersville to see."

Had someone seized the back of her neck? Her airway seemed compromised. Couldn't get enough oxygen. She counted to ten, willed herself to calm down. What the hell was he talking about?

She'd danced at Rachel's, that was all. An admirer talked her into a lap dance once. She'd taken his two hundred and sworn never to do it again. Wasn't worth it. She'd spent the whole time trying to keep his paws off her. She'd hardly danced at all. But she had a rule. No one touched the goods. She wasn't *that* desperate.

She steeled herself. "Look, it's no secret that I danced at Rachel's."

One side of his mouth rose and a huff of air escaped. "Danced? That's quite a euphemism, isn't it?"

"Danced." She gritted her teeth. "It wasn't the classiest job in the universe, but it paid the bills, and I saved up enough to start a new life. Anything wrong with that?"

"Nothing at all."

"Then why exactly are you here?"

"Because you did more than dance, Ambrosia. And I have proof."

She gulped. What the hell was he talking about?

"Ready to let me come in?"

"Absolutely not." She pushed him out the door.

"Fine. Give me about an hour to circulate these photos on the net."

Her throat constricted again. *Breathe, Amber, breathe.*

"What photos? I didn't do anything!"

"I've got photographic proof otherwise."

Curiosity got the best of her. Chad and Catie knew this guy. She felt sure she wasn't in any physical danger. Heck, if she didn't find out what was going on, she was liable to pass out from hyperventilation.

"Fine. Come in then. Let's see what you think you have."

He entered. "Nice place."

She scanned the room for a paper bag. There, on the table, holding lemons from the store. She dumped the lemons on the table and crunched the bag in her fist. "It's cozy. Now enough with the small talk. What do you want?"

"Look, I understand why you worked at Rachel's."

"For the money," she said, "pure and simple."

"I know that, and I understand. We all do what we have to do sometimes for the money."

"Do you have a point?"

"As a matter of fact, I do." He set his laptop on the table and sat down. "I want to show you a web site."

Her nerves skittered. Doctored photos, maybe? She hadn't the foggiest. Whatever it was, he wasn't going to get away with this.

"Shall we?" He pulled the other chair close beside him. "Have a seat so you can see."

She was too curious not to. He typed in some letters and a password, and photos of nude women popped onto the screen.

Truly, she told herself, *you have nothing to worry about. You didn't do anything wrong. You never posed for photos. The one lap dance you did was out in the open, not back in the private rooms. Nothing to worry about, Amber. Nothing.*

Until the first photo emerged.

Her bowels clenched and nausea gripped her throat. The blond girl with the slim muscular legs...legs famous for her pole dancing. That girl lay on a red satin sheet, her legs spread wide, another woman's head—Laura's head!—between them.

"It's enhanced," she whispered. "It can't be me."

"It is." Blake clicked on the screen. "And so is this."

This time she was on a man's lap, naked, her nipple between his lips. Her back arched and her eyes shut—clearly enjoying the stimulation.

She swallowed hard. "I'm going to throw up."

"I don't doubt it. Here's another."

This time she was giving a guy a blow job. Bitterness coated her tongue. She swallowed a heave.

"Seen enough?"

"It can't be. I never...posed for these. I don't understand."

"How many drugs did you do in your Rachel's days, Amber?"

"Damn it!" Tears welled in her eyes. "I didn't do any drugs! I hardly drank. It can't be me. It just can't be."

"This one will tell the tale I think."

A black-and-white photo appeared. Her ass was in the air, and a triangle shaped birthmark was apparent on her right butt cheek.

As if of its own accord, her right hand wandered to her hips, over the spot where her own birthmark marred her skin.

How could this be?

"How many more pictures are there?"

"There are twenty-four altogether. Six are girl/girl, two solo, the rest with men."

"Am I...having sex in any of them?"

"Alas, no. But you're doing pretty much everything else."

Her stomach threatened to empty. She covered her lips with her hand. "I don't understand."

"Neither do I. You seem like a nice girl."

"I really don't remember."

He powered down the laptop and flipped it closed. "I'm sure you don't. But unfortunately, that gets filed under the heading of 'not my problem.'"

"What do you mean?"

"What I mean is, I owe a bad man a lot of money. If I don't pay him soon, he's going to break my legs or worse."

God. He wanted money. Money to keep these photos out of the public eye. They were already on a web site. How many people had already seen them? Would it matter at this point?

"What web site are these on?"

"It's a private web site. Men pay top dollar to visit it."

"Where in hell did they get the pictures?"

"I haven't a clue. And I don't care. Like I said, I just need money."

She sighed. "And if you don't get it?"

"The good folks of Bakersville will get some brand new impressions of their reigning rodeo queen."

She clasped both sides of her head. To think she'd actually thought she could be happy here. That she could make a new start.

No such luck for Amber Cross. She was that lush Karen Hedstrom's trashy daughter. She always would be. Some things couldn't be escaped.

"How much do you need?" As if it mattered. She didn't have two dimes to spare.

"Twenty grand."

Icy fingers gripped her neck. "Twenty grand? You think I

have twenty grand? This is where I live, for God's sake, in this oversize closet!"

"Ambrosia—"

"*Don't* call me that!"

"I'm a reasonable man. I'll give you some time to get the money. You're a good friend of Catie McCray, and I happen to know she's loaded."

Catie? Seriously? She couldn't tell Catie about this.

"Your new boyfriend Harper's pretty well-off too."

She *really* couldn't tell Harper about this.

"Even Judy Williamson has managed to put away some money over the years."

Her boss? Was he kidding? She couldn't tell any of these people. She'd be run right out of town.

Where had those photos come from? She'd never done drugs, hardly ever drunk alcohol.

Except that one night when she blacked out.

Oh God.

She'd been at Rachel's for a few months, had gotten pretty popular, when two of the more experienced dancers invited her and Laura out after work one night. They went to their apartment. The bed had red satin sheets...

Oh my fucking God.

What was the woman's name? Megan? Martha? Something with an M. Were there photos of Laura too? Of course there were. She'd seen Laura's head between her own legs. She grabbed the laptop.

"Hey!" Blake said.

"Shut up, you creep. Let me see this. Get that web site back."

Surprisingly, he fired up the computer and brought it back

up. She grabbed it away from him, clicked on the home page, and found the index of the girls' names. Sure enough, Laura Lee. Laura still worked at Rachel's and probably had no idea she was all over this web site.

She shook her head. She felt for her friend, but right now Laura was the least of her worries.

"I don't have that kind of money."

"Like I said, I'm a reasonable man."

"What is this web site?"

"I told you. It's a paid site. Patrons of Rachel's can see the girls in action. Indulge their fantasies."

"How do you know about it?"

"I know people."

"Who?"

"Not your concern."

"I'd say it's very much my concern. What happens if I *do* pay you off? Then no one in Bakersville finds out about this. But I'm still plastered all over the net and anyone who pays for the privilege can see me in photos I had no idea I posed for."

"Again, not my problem."

She gulped and mustered all her strength. "It just might be, after all. Extortion happens to be a crime, you know."

"You think anyone will believe you? Look at your background, Amber. You were a stripper. You posed for photos."

She clenched both fists. "I did *not* pose for photos!"

"You can say that till the cows come home, but we have the physical evidence right here. Trust me, no one in Bakersville will know where these photos came from. They won't know they came from me. You can blab it all over town that Blake Buchanan tried to coerce you into paying him to keep the photos secret. Still, the photos speak for themselves. Do you think people will care whether I tried to get money out of you? Do you think they'll even believe it? Hell, no. They'll be too busy gossiping and sneaking looks at the goods. You'll be ruined in this town."

She shook her drooping head. He'd beaten her. "And every other town I try to escape to, I assume, unless you get your money."

"Now we're speaking the same language."

Tears rolled down her cheeks. "Why are you doing this?"

"Because I can. Because I need the money."

"I told you, I don't have it."

"You have a week." He turned off the laptop, closed it, stood, and walked to the door. "I'll be in touch."

Amber slammed the door, ran to the bathroom, and emptied her stomach.

CHAPTER NINE

Amber had been crying on her bed for an hour when her cell phone rang.

"Hey, baby, it's me."

Harper. She sniffed. "Hi there."

"Listen, I know this is short notice, but can you come to my place for dinner tonight?"

She was a mess and a half. She had to turn him down. "I'm sorry. I can't, Harper."

"Do you have other plans? If so, change them. This is worth your while, I promise."

An evening with Harper could do wonders for her, but it would only be a temporary fix. It pained her to turn him down. "I said I can't."

"Baby, what's wrong? You sound all nasal."

"I'm fine. It's just...allergies. Terrible hay fever."

What a stupid lie. But maybe he'd buy it.

"Take an antihistamine then. And get yourself all prettied up and come to my place for dinner."

Can't he take a hint? "Harper, if you want sex, I don't think—"

He laughed. "Of course I want sex, Amber. You're hot, and I like you. But that's not what this is about. Just say you'll come. Please?"

"I really can't."

"You won't regret it, I promise."

Of course she wouldn't regret it. She'd never regret spending time with him. But she was screwed up right now. Her eyes were swollen and her nose red. She glanced at the clock beside her bed. Two.

"What time?"

"How does six sound?"

Four hours. Could she get herself together in that amount of time? God knew she needed something to get her mind off the mess she was in. She couldn't accomplish anything toward her goal of twenty grand on a Sunday evening. Why not spend it with Harper?

"Okay, I'll be there."

"Great! I can't wait to see you. Bye now."

"Bye."

She turned her head back into her pillow and cried some more.

★ ★ ★

An hour later she steeled herself and rose from the bed. A quick look in her bathroom mirror and she considered calling Harper to cancel. She looked like death, to put it bluntly. Not death warmed over.

Just death.

Her eyes were red and puffy, her cheeks and hair matted with tears and snot, her skin pasty and gray, her nose so red she could double as Rudolph.

Like an idiot, she'd neglected to get the web site information and password from Blake Buchanan, so she couldn't do any research on her little problem. He hadn't left a number, just said he'd be in touch.

Asshole.

She turned on the shower and cranked the water as hot as it would go. She needed heat, and then she'd splash her face with cold when she got out. Hopefully that would avert some of the swelling.

She washed her hair twice and conditioned it with a hot oil treatment. When she dried off and looked at her face, she was pleasantly surprised. She splashed several handfuls of cold water over it, and she looked almost normal. Eye drops got rid of the red eyes. Her eyelids were still slightly swollen, but probably not noticeable to anyone who didn't know to look for it. Now if she could just keep from crying until after she got home from Harper's.

That's all it took—just that one thought and tears started to flow. She gulped them away. Nope. Had to stay strong at least for tonight. Heck, for tomorrow too. She had to go into work. She needed all the money she could make right now.

She dried her hair and pulled it into a high ponytail. The stretch would make her face look less cried out. Well, it was a thought anyway. She put on just a touch of makeup and lipstick.

She dressed in a denim miniskirt and silk blouse. She slid on navy mules and pronounced herself fit—as well as could be expected—for human eyes.

She had an hour before she needed to leave, so she got her tablet out and Googled Rachel's. Time to find out what might be going on.

Marta. That was the woman's name. She was European—German, or Austrian. Amber never knew which one. She went only by Marta. She wasn't stuck with a stupid stage name like Ambrosia Love.

Maybe she didn't need one.

She wore leather and furs and diamonds, all gifts from the men she serviced, Amber had assumed at the time. Now she wasn't so sure. Perhaps she made her own money...by luring unsuspecting new young strippers to her place to get drunk and have their photos taken.

Amber shook her head. Surely alcohol couldn't have been responsible for this. She and Laura must have been drugged. But with what?

Tears threatened again, and she clicked off her tablet. No use crying over spilled milk, or alcohol, or whatever they'd given her.

Damn it, I want a nice evening with Harper. And she would have it. She could lose it tomorrow.

She had no doubt she would.

Her body remained tense during the half-hour drive to Harper's ranch house. She tried breathing in through her mouth, out through her nose, and finally gave up. Relaxation wasn't to be.

Tonight she might forego her two drink minimum. Some alcohol might be just what she needed.

Course she really didn't want to go there. Not with the genes she carried inside her. And certainly not with what she'd just learned had happened one of the two times she'd allowed herself to get drunk.

She'd have a nice glass of wine. Harper liked wine and he seemed to know a little bit about it. She'd had half a glass with him last night, after all. And that was after she'd had two cosmos at the party.

Course it was a lot later that she had the wine, so she hadn't really violated her own rule.

One glass of wine. Hopefully it would relax her.

Maybe with a valium chaser?

Sheesh.

She drove onto the Cha Cha ranch property and followed the directions Harper had given her. Soon his ranch house came into view. She liked his house. It wasn't huge and sprawling like his mother's a few miles away, or Catie's that she shared with Chad.

Modest was nice. More her style.

She parked, walked to the door, and knocked.

Harper opened it, looking just as tousled and sexy as he always did. How did his hair always look so charmingly disheveled? It just begged her to run her fingers through it. His muscular rancher's body looked heavenly in jeans and a black western shirt.

McCray boys be damned. Harper Bay was the most handsome man in Bakersville.

"Hey, baby. It's great to see you." He pulled her close and gave her a smoldering kiss.

The familiar jolts coursed through her. God, this man affected her like no one else.

"So what's the big surprise?" she asked.

"What makes you think there's a surprise? Maybe I just wanted to have dinner with you."

His eyes gleamed. Mischief. He was up to no good.

"Stop kidding around, Harp. I've had a day and a half."

"You have? What's wrong, baby?"

Aw hell, what'd I go and say that for? She sure didn't want to get into that with him. Not tonight. "Oh, just my allergies and all."

"I didn't know you had allergies."

That was because she didn't. "Just some hay fever. It acts

up now and then."

He took her hand. "So what did you do today?"

"Other than sneeze my ass off? Just went to the grocery store." *And got blackmailed. Nothing much.*

"Would you like a drink? I learned how to make a cosmo just for you."

"Did you?" *God, he's sweet.*

"Yup. Got one all ready for you. I even tasted it, and you know what? It's not half bad."

"Of course not. Do you think I'd drink something bad?"

He furrowed his brow. "It's pink, Amber."

She let out a laugh. "That's the splash of cranberry, genius."

"Yes, I know that. It's just, I never thought a pink drink would taste good. But it's pretty good."

"It's basically a vodka martini with some triple sec and a splash of cranberry juice, Harp. It's not all that girly of a drink."

"Yeah, but it's pink."

She shook her head, smiling. "So you've mentioned."

He handed her the drink. "Aren't you having one?"

"I don't do pink drinks." He grinned.

"What are you having then?"

"A vodka martini."

She laughed again. "You're too funny. So are you going to tell me what my surprise is?"

"It'll be here soon."

"Oh." She perked up. Granted, she'd had a shit day, but she was like a little girl when it came to surprises. She loved getting presents. Always had. She'd gotten darn few in her lifetime. She took a sip of her drink. "Not bad, cowboy, for your first time."

"Thank you." He waggled his eyebrows at her.

Damn, he was good-looking. Shudders ran down her spine and settled between her legs. She hadn't thought it possible to get turned on tonight, after the day she'd had. But Harper Bay could do it to her.

"Go on out to the deck and have a seat," he said. "I thought we'd eat outside. It's such a warm night for the end of April."

"Sounds good." Actually it sounded great. Amber loved the outdoors, and Colorado was such a beautiful state.

"I'll be out in a minute. I want to take care of a few things."

"Okay." She went outside and stood on the deck, inhaling the fresh evening air. The peaks of the Rockies glowed violet and indigo against the azure sky spotted with fluffy clouds. The sun was an orange ball sitting atop the snowcapped mountains. She inhaled again, ignoring the aroma of cow that crept by.

She took a seat at his patio table. It was set for three.

Three?

So her surprise was a person?

Who could it be?

Before she had time to think, the French doors opened with a squeak behind her. She stood and turned to see Harper and a nice-looking older man with dirty blond hair and golden eyes.

Harper's dark eyes sparkled. "Amber, I'd like you to meet Thunder Morgan."

CHAPTER TEN

Amber's pulse pounded inside her head. *What the fuck has he done?* She was in no condition to meet her birth father. She'd just been blackmailed, for God's sake. To be fair, Harper didn't know that, but still, he was interfering in something that wasn't his business. Who did he think he was, anyway?

"Harper"—she forced a smile—"may I see you inside for a moment?"

"What's up?"

She steadied her breathing, afraid she might lose control. "Just something I need to get your opinion on in the kitchen. You don't mind, do you, Mr. Morgan?"

"Not at all."

She clenched her teeth. Could this day get any worse? "We'll only be a minute."

She dragged Harper through the kitchen and out into the living room where she could be sure Thunder Morgan wouldn't hear them.

"What in God's name were you thinking?"

"Relax." He pushed a strand of hair behind her ear. "I didn't tell him anything. I just gave him a call when I got back home this morning and found out he was in Denver for a few weeks. So I invited him up for dinner. He's a great guy. I want you to get to know him."

Amber stared at him. He was actually serious. "And exactly what do you propose I say to him? 'Hi, I'm the daughter you never knew you had?'"

"Of course not. As far as he knows, at least for tonight, you're my friend. My date. Whatever you want to be."

"What I want to be is not here."

"Amber, come on. I didn't tell him your last name, so no worries. I thought you'd be happy to meet him."

"You caught me off guard, Harper. Jesus! Don't you think I might have liked a little time to prepare for this?"

"If I had given you time to prepare for it you would have freaked out."

"Uh...yeah. Kind of like I'm doing now?"

"I mean you would have freaked yourself out into a frenzy before he ever go here. Now you can just go with the flow."

She paced around his Berber carpet, sure she was wearing tracks in it. "Does this look like a person who's going with the flow?"

"Calm down, baby. You're going to get along great."

"So I'm just supposed to—what?—talk about *what* exactly? What do I have to say to a bronc buster?"

"You're the rodeo queen. You have a lot in common. You represent the rodeo."

Yeah, the rodeo queen. If Blake Buchanan had anything to say about it, she'd be dethroned in a week's time.

"And a few days ago you talked about learning barrel racing."

She rubbed her temples. Her interest in barrel racing seemed like a lifetime ago. Yet he was right. It had only been a few days ago. Why, oh why, had she ever wanted to race? If she hadn't, Catie wouldn't have introduced her to Blake Buchanan, and he wouldn't have recognized her from Rachel's and started snooping around on the Internet.

What if, what if, what if?

What if her mother hadn't kicked her out? What if she'd been able to get work doing nails and had never gone to Rachel's?

She sighed. Life was full of "what ifs."

"Amber"—Harper traced her lower lip with his finger—"I'm sorry if this isn't a surprise you particularly wanted. I thought you'd be happy. I wouldn't do anything to make you unhappy."

"I know that."

"But I invited him here. He's a friend of my family. And right now we're being rude."

She nodded. "You're right, of course. I'm sorry. I just wish I knew what to say."

"You're good with people. I'll start him talking, and then you just pop into the conversation when you're ready, okay?"

"Sure, I can do that." She let out a breath. "I guess it's now or never then."

"Come on." He took her hand. "You'll be great."

★ ★ ★

Thunder Morgan had led an interesting life, traveling the rodeo circuit. He'd even done German rodeos for a while. He had a wonderful sense of humor, and soon Amber was laughing until tears formed in her eyes.

Her eyes.

They were almost identical to his.

Did he notice?

"Did you ever regret not settling down?" she asked.

"Well, not overly," he said. "Sure, it would have been nice

to have a wife to come home to and kids to carry on the name, but would it have been fair to them? Would it be fair to a wife to never be home, to never help her with the kids? Would it be fair to the kids to have to grow up without a father?"

A lump formed in Amber's throat. "I see what you mean."

"I was a traveler. For a while I didn't keep a permanent residence at all. I just hit circuit after circuit, winning purse after purse, putting away what I could for a rainy day. When you're in the rodeo, you know you can't do it forever. It's kind of like pro football. Your body eventually says no more."

"Seems you had quite a good run," Harper said.

"Yup, a sight better than most."

"Do you keep a permanent residence now?" Amber asked.

"Sure do. On the western slope. Not too far from Harper's ranch out there."

"I told you that Thunder used to work at Bay Crossing, didn't I?" Harper said.

"Yes, of course," Amber said. "That's how you know him."

"Nothing like the western slope," Thunder said. "I love it here, don't get me wrong. And I've seen some wonderful places during my travels, but I always knew when it came time to retire, I'd be back on the slope with the peaches and apple orchards and vineyards. I'm looking into winemaking now."

Harper raised his eyebrows. "Really? I didn't know that."

"Gotta do something to keep busy," Thunder said. "It drives me crazy to sit around doing nothing."

"Me too," Amber said. "I'm always finding something to do on my time off."

"What do you do, pretty lady?"

"I'm a manicurist."

"You don't say? My mother was a manicurist. Small

world."

Not that small. Manicurists were a dime a dozen, but Amber didn't say that. Instead, she found herself feeling closer to him, wondering if her interest in doing nails came from his mother.

She let out a huff of air and hoped neither of them noticed. She was grasping at straws. She'd decided to learn nails because the vocational high school offered it, and she'd have a skill with which to make a living. She didn't have some huge dream to be a manicurist. She was good at it, true, but was it her life's work? No.

If she could do whatever she wanted, she'd ride horses. That was what she loved.

And maybe *that* was from her father. She smiled.

"You look happy," Harper said.

Happy? Meeting her real father, finding out her love of horses might have come from him? It sure hadn't come from her mother. Karen wouldn't know a horse from a cat. Yes, happy was a nice word. A glowing warmth caressed her skin. For a moment she'd forgotten about her ill-fated meeting with Blake Buchanan earlier.

Damn. Had to think about that.

"I'm doing all right," she said. She turned back to Thunder Morgan. "Tell me about your place on the slope."

"It's a ranch house on about a hundred acres. I don't need a lot of space for just me and a couple horses and a couple dogs. I have neighbors who care for the animals while I'm away."

"When do you plan to start making wine?"

"I have to find a vineyard first. There are a couple small ones for sale. I'm looking into it. I have a little nest egg. Bronc bustin' paid the bills. It didn't make me rich, that's for sure, but

I can afford a small operation."

"What kind of wine do you want to make?"

"Red, definitely. I'm partial to Rhone blends. You know—syrah, grenache, mourvedre."

Amber shook her head. "You'll have to excuse me. I was telling Harper just yesterday that I know absolutely nothing about wine. I like the taste of most of it, though. Especially reds."

"I have a great little Rhone blend we can try tonight with our steaks," Harper said, rising. "I'll get it. And Amber baby, you'll get your steak blue tonight."

"You like your steak blue?" Thunder smiled. "A girl who likes her meat still mooing is a girl after my own heart."

★ ★ ★

"I can't believe you did that," Amber said after Thunder left, "but I'm glad you did. He's amazing."

"And he's your dad."

She shook her head. "I wouldn't have believed it, except for the eyes. I'm a dead ringer for Karen otherwise. But those eyes of his. It was like staring into my own."

"So, baby, when are you going to tell him?"

"Tell him what? That he's my dad?" She scoffed. "I think around the fifth of never."

"You can't be serious."

"Of course I am. He's got a life, Harper. A life that doesn't include a twenty-two-year-old daughter he never knew he had. He'll probably think I'm lying. I doubt he even remembers my mother."

"You said so yourself. The eyes tell all."

"Yes, but other than the eyes I don't look a thing like him."

"There's DNA testing."

"I couldn't ask him to do that."

"Why not? If he doesn't believe you, that's the one way to know for sure. For both of you."

"He's such a nice guy. I don't want to screw up his life."

"Who says you'll screw it up? He never married. He's retired now. He's all alone. He might welcome the idea of family."

Would he? Amber's heart did a flip-flop. It was possible. She sure loved the idea herself. She hadn't spoken to Karen in over six years. While she finished school, Laura had been her family. Laura's mother hadn't been around all that much, and once they'd both graduated, she very nicely told them to get the hell out. At Rachel's the girls were her family, with Marta as a mother figure.

Marta.

Some mother figure, drugging girls and exploiting them.

Blake Buchanan and those horrible Internet images catapulted into her mind. Her tummy—full of blue rib eye, tomato-and-mozzarella salad, loaded baked potato, and green beans—threatened to betray her.

Escape. She longed for escape. And there sat Harper, his dark eyes smoking, his hair tousled and sexy as usual, smiling with those full pink lips surrounding nearly perfect white teeth. One of his front teeth slightly overlapped the other. A tiny imperfection that made him even sexier. Her heart melted.

He'd done something so wonderful for her tonight. He'd found her father and brought him to her.

So a man wasn't in her immediate future. At least that's what she'd thought. Maybe she'd rethink her stance.

He wanted her. Even now, just sitting on the couch, electricity sizzled between them. His finger brushing her forearm sent tiny flames igniting over her whole body.

Her need was more than physical, though. She liked him. Liked how he treated her, liked his openness, his forthrightness, how he'd told her in no uncertain terms he wanted to take her to bed. It was a statement of pure honesty. Who couldn't respect a man who valued honesty above all else?

She liked his family, liked his place, liked pretty much everything about him. Loved that he'd offered to bring her breakfast this morning.

Loved that he'd brought her father to her.

Loved.

She was falling for Harper Bay.

Damn it.

His arms would be paradise—a whimsical escape from Blake Buchanan and his threats.

How she longed for escape. Escape only Harper could give her.

His deep voice interrupted her racing thoughts. "Don't you think?"

"Think what?"

"That Thunder might welcome the idea of family at this point in his life?"

His beautiful eyes, crinkling in the corners, ensnared her. "I suppose he might."

She melted into his arms.

When their lips met, all doubts rinsed from her mind. Her body took over. She wanted to make love with Harper. She would not stop like she had last night.

He traced the outside of her lips with his soft probing

tongue. A butterfly kiss. Laura had taught her about that back in high school, after Karen had kicked her out. She'd never experienced one until now.

The kiss warmed her, heated her, turned her into a blistering inferno. Had she not known better she'd have been convinced her skin was glowing red with passion. Harper replaced the tip of his tongue with his teeth, and he nibbled gently over her upper lip, her lower, and sucked the lower lip into his mouth.

Amber sighed. Goosebumps erupted over her flesh. How was it possible to feel so hot yet so cold at one time? A soft moan met her ears.

It took a moment to realize it had come from her own throat.

"I love kissing you, baby," Harper whispered against her mouth. "You're so soft and sweet, so responsive." He parted the seam of her lips with his tongue and eased it inside.

If she'd had any shred of resistance left, his tongue erased it. She bathed herself in the kiss, let it consume her. Her tongue met his with passion so powerful she thought she might explode with desire and lust.

They ravaged each other's mouths. Amber touched Harper's cheek, and his stubble scraped against her fingers and palm. So masculine, so right. He was so handsome, beautifully sculpted, and she wanted him so much. Her heart beat against her sternum so hard and fast she felt sure he could feel it in his own chest.

And still they kissed. His hands wandered over her shoulders, her arms, until they found her breasts. Her nipples tightened and budded against the fabric of her bra. They ached for his mouth, his tongue.

"Please, Harper, make love to me."

Had those words come from her mouth? Yes they had, and she meant them with all her soul.

"Oh, baby." The deep timbre of his voice vibrated over her. "I want you so much."

He rose and took her hand, led her upstairs to a large master bedroom. A four poster king-size bed draped in a mahogany comforter sat against one wall.

He turned to her, his eyes smoldering. "Are you sure this time?"

Her clit throbbed with each beat of her heart. "I'm sure, Harper. Take me to bed."

He gently led her to the bed and eased her down upon the silky covers. "You're so beautiful, Amber."

Her skin warmed. His words touched her heart, her soul. She knew she was attractive. Those years at Rachel's had proved that. But to hear it from Harper's full lips that had already given her so much pleasure was nirvana.

He slowly undressed her, discarded her blouse and her bra, and feasted on her nipples.

Sweet ecstasy. His mouth felt so good on her breasts, so good and so right. Her areolas wrinkled, pushing her nipples out farther, sending tingles to her core.

She'd had some experience—not a lot, but some—but never had she known a man who could drive her as crazy as this one.

"Your breasts are delicious," he said.

He moved downward and deftly removed her skirt and panties. She started to kick off her mules, but he stopped her.

"Leave them on. You look amazing."

She wanted to please him, truly she did, but leaving them

on reminded her too much of her days at Rachel's. She didn't want anything to taint this night. She kicked them off anyway, hoping he wouldn't notice.

He looked down, frowned slightly, but said nothing.

And into her mind came a single thought. *He understood.* She knew he did.

He spread her legs and smiled. "I can't wait to taste you again."

She tried to stop him, or she at least thought about it. He'd given her so much pleasure this morning that she wanted to please him first.

But when his tongue touched her hard bud, she was lost. He feasted on her folds, her clit, all of her, his stubble grazing over her and making her hotter. She shuddered. Had anything in the world ever felt as good as this?

Her hips rose, thrust against his mouth, urging him to delve deeper into her wetness. Her naked body tingled against his fully clothed one.

"You're wearing too many clothes, cowboy."

"Shh," he said against her, his voice a soft vibration against her slick folds. "I'm busy."

Far be it from her to bother a busy man. She reached forward, grabbed two fistfuls of his silky hair, and pulled him farther into her heat.

"God, that feels amazing." When had her voice lowered an octave?

He held her at bay for what seemed like an eternity, until she couldn't help but shout at him. "Please, you've got to let me come!"

He thrust two fingers inside her, and she shattered. Up she flew to the highest peaks of the Rockies. Her entire body throbbed along with her sex, and when she floated downward, his fingers still moved in and out of her, gently now, softly.

So good. So very good.

He lowered his head, but she stopped him. "Oh no, not this time."

"You didn't like?" His devilish smile told her he knew otherwise.

"Are you kidding? You're the most talented man in the world at that."

"High praise."

"Indeed. But it's my turn. There are a few things I'm pretty good at too."

She pulled him down on the bed and maneuvered on top of him. His erection pulsed against her naked wet sex. How she wanted him. She was ready to yank down his pants and mount him then and there.

But no. She wanted to please him first, as he'd pleased her. She unbuttoned his shirt slowly, all the while trailing light kisses over his neck and chest. His copper coin nipples stuck out through chestnut chest hair. They were turgid, begging to be sucked. She obliged.

"Oh, baby, you have no idea how good that feels."

She chuckled against his warm flesh. "I think I have a vague concept."

"I know... I just...my nipples are really sensitive. More so than most guys, I think. At least that's what women say."

She let his nipple tumble from her lips and looked up. "You've had a lot of women, huh?"

His eyes were heavy, half-lidded. "Not a lot. A few. They've all been amazed at how my nipples react."

"I see." She placed a soft kiss on one nipple. "They're

delicious, actually."

"I'm glad, baby, because you can keep doing that forever and I won't complain."

"With pleasure." She sucked and tugged, moving from nipple to nipple and loving every second of it.

Harper squirmed beneath her, his jean-clad erection pushing against her.

She wanted to see him naked. In all his tousled sexy glory. She let his nipple go and rained tiny kisses down his chest, his belly, pausing to lick his belly button. With precision, she unsnapped and unzipped his jeans.

Lord. No underwear.

"Commando? Expecting to get lucky tonight?"

"Just hoping, baby, that's all."

His erection sprang free from a nest of brown curls. He was magnificent, large and golden, with a drop of fluid glistening on the head of his cock. She licked it off.

He shuddered beneath her.

"You like that?"

"God, baby, yes. Suck me. Please."

"Since you said please." She twirled her tongue around the swollen head and savored the salty masculine flavor. He groaned in pleasure. She warmed, and her own sex throbbed.

Pleasing him pleased her. More than it had with any other man she'd been with.

She continued her assault, trailing her tongue along his length to his base and back up again, teasing and teasing, until she finally lowered her mouth and took all of him to the back of her throat.

"Ah, God, baby," he groaned. "Yes, take it all."

She could do this for hours, suck his beautiful cock. She

wanted this as much as he did.

Surprising. She'd never enjoyed this aspect of sex much.

Until now.

Until now when she was with a man she truly cared about.

When had she started caring this much? When had she fallen in love?

Don't go there, Amber.

She resumed her task, loving every delicious moment of it.

"Baby, baby..."

She lifted her head. "Yeah?"

"Nightstand drawer. Condom."

God, yes. Condom. She wanted him inside her. She grappled in the drawer and retrieved a foil packet. Quickly she ripped it open, sheathed him, climbed atop him, and sank herself onto his hardness.

Had she ever felt so full? So complete?

Slowly she moved up and down, finding his rhythm, letting his own pistoning hips guide her.

"Yeah, baby. God, yeah." His voice was deep, and his tone seemed to be hugging her, urging her to make love to him. "Fuck me. That's it."

Not a word she liked. But he said it so sweetly that it turned her on even more. She wanted to fuck him. She wanted to fuck his brains out. Her whole body felt like a rocket ready to launch.

She moved faster. Her clit rubbed against him as she pumped, and oh, oh...*yes*. The orgasm hit her with more force than she was prepared for, and she nearly fell off the bed.

His strong hands steadied her. "That's right, baby. Come for me. Come."

The climaxes kept coming and coming. His hips gyrated harder up into her.

"Harper, so many, God...God, yes!"

"Yeah, baby. I'm going to come." He thrust up into her faster. "Yes, yes, baby."

As he spilled into her, her orgasms slowed. She fell forward onto his chest, their perspiration mingling into a scent of musky completion. She inhaled against his neck. Mmm. Their own special aroma. Perfect.

"Oh, baby," he growled. "That was amazing."

She nodded against his neck. Couldn't bring herself to speak yet.

"Amber."

She drew all her strength and sent it to her vocal cords. "Hmm?"

"Stay with me. Spend the night."

She snuggled against him, already half-asleep.

CHAPTER ELEVEN

"Rise and shine." Harper's voice cut through Amber's dream of lovemaking.

She opened her eyes. "Hey. What time is it?"

"Six. I gotta get moving. Ranches don't run themselves."

"Yeah. I'm working today too. My first client's at eight, so I need to go."

"Time for breakfast?"

"I wish I could. I have to get home and shower and change."

He grinned. "You could shower here."

She could...

Images of Harper's manly body covered in droplets of warm water enticed her, but... "Ha. Then I'd never leave. But I'll take a rain check on the shower."

"I'll hold you to that. Do you have time for a quick cup of coffee?"

"Only if it's to go. Sorry."

"Okay. I'll get you one." He leaned down and gave her a light kiss on the lips. "Last night was wonderful, baby. Thank you."

Thank you? No man had ever thanked her for sex before. Should she thank him back?

"Um...you're welcome?"

He chuckled. "You are priceless, Amber. I never would have thought you were my type, but damn, I love being with you."

Not his type? Was that an insult? "What do you mean by that?"

"Just...you're not like the country girls I grew up with. You're more sophisticated. You look different. You act different. I mean, I always thought you were beautiful. I just had no idea I'd like you so much."

He hadn't hedged for words, thank God. "So that was a compliment then?"

He laughed again. "Of course it was."

"Good. 'Cause I like you too. And last night was amazing for me as well." She got up and started collecting her clothes.

"I'll get your coffee, baby. Meet me down in the kitchen."

★ ★ ★

"Angie, when are you and Rafe going back to the slope?"

"Tomorrow. Why?"

Amber sighed as she clipped the cuticles on Angie's right hand. "I need to talk to someone."

"I've got all day today. I want to go see Violet this afternoon, but other than that I'm free."

"I've got a full schedule today," Amber said. "Can we have dinner?"

"Sure. Why don't Rafe and I meet you at the Blue Bird?"

She exhaled a long breath. "Well...I was kind of hoping we could talk alone. Nothing against Rafe but—"

"Girl talk?"

She had no idea. "Yeah, something like that."

"How about lunch?"

"I can't take lunch. I'm booked through. Please? It's important."

"Of course. Rafe'll understand. The Blue Bird?"

"My place, actually. I need privacy."

Angie's hand stiffened under Amber's ministrations. "Amber? What on earth is going on?"

Amber looked down, unable to meet her friend's gaze. Would Angie believe her? Would she understand? Angie had her own skeletons, so she was Amber's safest bet. Catie was busy with the new baby, and Judy was her boss, for goodness' sake. She wasn't that close to anyone else yet, at least not enough to trust with this. "I'll tell you tonight. God, I really need to talk to someone."

"Okay. Tonight at your place. You're obviously distraught. I'll get take out from the Blue Bird and bring it over. Say six?"

"Six thirty."

★ ★ ★

"No offense, Amber, but you look like hell."

Amber held her door open and Angie walked in, carrying a takeout bag from the Blue Bird and a bottle of wine. "Good to see you too, Ang."

Angie made herself at home in Amber's small abode, setting food on the table and grabbing two plates out of the cupboard. "Come on and sit. There's obviously something you need to spill. Where's your corkscrew?"

"Top drawer." Amber plunked down at the table and thunked her head on the hard surface. "God, where to start?"

A soft pop met her ears—the wine cork.

"I can't hear you when you're talking into the table, hon."

She lifted her head and sighed.

"So does this have to do with my brother?" Angie poured

two glasses of wine.

Harper? He was the least of her worries, except he'd want nothing to do with her when he found out the other issues she was dealing with. Amber shook her head. "No. I mean, not really."

"Seems you two are getting along pretty well."

"We are. I'm surprised, to be honest."

Angie laughed. "So is he. Never in a million years did he think you were his type."

So she'd heard. "Have you talked to him about us?"

"Not really. He just said he likes you a lot and he's looking forward to seeing where it goes."

She nodded. She felt the same. He knew more about her than she'd let on to anyone so far in Bakersville, and he wasn't judging her. Course the relationship wouldn't go much further if she couldn't keep Blake Buchanan at bay.

Stripping at Rachel's was one thing. Pornographic photos on the net were something else entirely.

"I like him too." She sighed. "A lot." Big understatement.

Angie took a sip of wine and began to take the cartons out of the Blue Bird sack. "So what's the problem then?"

"With Harper? There is none." At least not yet.

"Okay. What else is going on? There's a new guy in your life. You should be shining like the sun. Instead you look like you've been reincarnated as a rag."

She couldn't crack a smile. "Damn, Angie. You cut right to the chase, don't you?"

"I try."

Amber let out a controlled breath. *Here goes nothing.* "I haven't told you much about my life in San Antonio."

"No, you haven't. Every time I've asked you've changed

the subject."

"You're right, and I'm sorry. It's not a time in my life I like to talk about. Or even think about for that matter."

"Well, you did tell me about your two one-night stands." She winked.

True, she had. About seven months ago, before Angie and Rafe had hooked up. Angie had said she needed some sex, and Amber had suggested a one-night stand. Who would've thought two one-night stands would turn out to be the tamest things she'd done in San Antonio?

Amber picked up her wine glass and took a long sip. "I guess it's best to start at the beginning."

For the next hour, she poured out her whole sordid story, beginning with being kicked out of Karen's house to leaving San Antonio.

Angie listened with rapt attention, her green eyes wide. "And Harp knows all of this?"

"All of what I've told you so far."

Angie smiled and patted Amber's forearm. "My brother's a good man."

Her friend's touch soothed her...but only a little. "That he is."

"If he's okay with all of this, why are you so upset?"

Those same icy fingers gripped the back of her neck. "Because I haven't told you everything yet. I've only told what... what I remember."

"Sorry, babe. Not following here."

"Oh God." She pushed her wine glass ahead of her. "Is there any more?"

"Yeah." Angie poured another glass. "I've never seen you drink more than two drinks."

"This is only my second."

"I know. I'm just saying."

Amber took a sip. It was a nice red, kind of spicy. She'd hoped to learn more about wine from Harper. She'd hoped for so much...

"You know that guy who used to work for Chad? Blake Buchanan?"

"Yeah."

"You've lived here most of your life. You already know the story about him and the librarian."

Angie nodded. "Heck, that's old news. Evie's over it. I thought the whole town was."

"Maybe they are. I don't know."

"He seems like a nice enough guy to me."

Amber widened her eyes. Seriously? Angie couldn't see through the jerk? She was as blind as Catie. "He's not a nice guy, Ang."

"Oh? Why do you say that?"

Amber swallowed the lump in her throat. "He's blackmailing me."

Angie nearly spat wine across the table. "Say what?"

"Did I stutter? He's blackmailing me."

"How?"

"Turns out he was in San Antonio for a while, and he remembers me from Rachel's."

"So what? If Harper knows, and I know, and we're fine with that, what makes you think everyone else won't be fine with it?"

"I'm rodeo queen, for one thing. Hardly a job for a stripper." She clutched the stem of her goblet. "But that's not the issue."

"What is, then?"

Amber gulped down the last of her wine. *Damn.* She'd met her two drink max. She could use another.

She swallowed, her tummy fluttering. Angie was her friend. She would understand. Wouldn't she?

She cleared her throat. "Blake Buchanan came by yesterday with some photos on the Internet."

"Photos of you?"

She nodded. "They were definitely me. Thing is, I have no memory of posing for them at all. I found my roommate Laura on the web site too, and I know she'd never pose either."

"Nude photos?"

She had no idea. "Yeah. More than just nude photos. I'm doing things in them."

Angie's eyes widened. "You're doing...*it?*"

"Not *it*, in the literal sense, but pretty much everything but."

Angie paused. A long pause. Then, "But how? If you don't remember... I don't understand, Amber."

"Neither did I at first, but I'm pretty sure I was drugged. I seriously have no memory of the whole thing."

"What web site is it?"

"It's an expensive paid web site for Rachel's patrons, as far as I can tell."

"Do you have the URL?"

"No. He didn't give it to me, and I didn't think to ask for it." Why hadn't she gotten the damn URL? "I wasn't thinking at all. This came at me from left field."

"I understand. Do you have any idea how this happened?"

"I have a hunch. There was a woman at Rachel's—her name was Marta. She was kind of our mother hen. One night she invited Laura and me to her place. We got to drinking...and I blacked out. I've only been drunk twice in my life. The other was when I had the first one-night stand that I told you about. Anyway, I recognized the bed at her place from the photos."

"You think you were drugged?"

"I can't see any other explanation. I was obviously awake in the pictures. Something had to make me forget. I assumed I was drunk and I blacked out. Now I'm not so sure."

"Something to induce amnesia—"

"Exactly."

"Like the date rape drug, maybe?"

"Maybe. I have no idea. Do I look like I have a clue about drugs? I never did any of them. Hell, even if I'd wanted to, I couldn't afford them."

Angie squeezed her forearm. "Honey, I know. I'm not accusing you of doing drugs."

"I know. I'm sorry."

"No need to apologize."

Amber choked out a sob. "Blake wants twenty grand in a week or he goes public with the photos."

Angie raised her eyebrows. "Twenty grand?"

"Yes. I told him there's no way I can get it, but he says that's not his problem."

"Well, there's no problem." Angie patted her arm. "I'll give you the money."

Amber sighed. What a wonderful friend. "Angie, that's not why I wanted to talk to you."

"I know that, honey. I know that. But you need help, and I have the means to help you."

"But don't you see? If we give him the money, he'll just keep holding the photos over my head. When he needs more money, guess where he'll go? And in the meantime my photos are on the Internet! Without my permission. Hell, without my knowledge!"

Angie scooted her chair closer and wrapped her arms around Amber in a tight hug. "We'll figure this out, I promise."

"I hope you're right."

"I want you to listen to me. There's someone who can help you."

"Who?"

Angie let out an exhale. "You won't like it."

"I'll try anything at this point."

"Harper. You have to tell Harper."

CHAPTER TWELVE

"Are you crazy?" No way was she telling Harper. He'd never forgive her.

"He's a lawyer, Amber. He can help."

"Things are going well with us. I don't want to risk that."

"Don't you see? Harper cares about you. He won't let anyone hurt you. And he can help. These photos are up without your permission. That's not legal."

She gulped. "I know that. But what can I do?"

Angie grasped her hand. "You can tell Harper, and we can go from there."

Amber's head jarred at the ring of her cell phone. She didn't recognize the number.

"Hello?"

"Hello, darlin'. It's Blake."

Blake Buchanan. Her body stiffened. "It's him," she mouthed to Angie.

"What do you want?"

"Just checkin' in. Seeing how things are going. I know you're dining with your friend Angelina Bay Grayhawk. And I know she's loaded. Did you get my money yet?"

Nausea seized her. He was out there. Watching her. How dare he violate her that way?

She nearly laughed out loud. He'd clearly already thrown caution to the wind by blackmailing her. There wasn't much he wouldn't do, was there?

"Don't call me again."

"Hey, I'm just looking out for both of us. The sooner I get my money, the sooner I'm outta your hair, and you can go on with your life."

Anger boiled in her belly. "Don't you dare patronize me. Say you get your money. What then? You haven't given me the web site URL. For all I know the photos will still be there and you'll come back to me the next time you find yourself strapped for cash."

"Hey, the deal was you get me twenty grand and I don't divulge this information to the sainted town of Bakersville. There was nothing more than that."

"So my photos stay on the web site then? You want me to pay twenty grand for that?"

"That's your only choice for now. I have no power to get the photos down."

"Then what good are you?" She clicked the phone off.

"You're just going to piss him off," Angie said.

Tears streamed down her cheeks. "I don't give a damn!"

But she did. That was a lie. She didn't want to be ruined in Bakersville. She loved it here. She'd finally found a place that felt like home. She'd found friends. She'd even found a man. A man who felt like home.

Maybe he'd understand. Angie thought so.

Angie took both her hands. "Go to the bathroom and get cleaned up. We're going to go see my brother."

★ ★ ★

"Harper, you're not being fair."

Harper paced up and down. "Fair?" He glared at his sister.

"None of this is fair."

"You're absolutely right," Angie said. "But it's the most unfair to Amber."

He looked over at the woman—the beautiful woman he'd begun to think of as his—and his heart broke. He could handle that she'd been a stripper, that she'd been kicked out of her house by a drunken mother and she had to find a way to earn a living. That was admirable. Noble even.

But the photos?

True, she claimed to have no knowledge of their existence prior to yesterday. Could he believe her? He wanted to, but evidence pointed against her. By her own admission, she was awake and fully active in the photos.

And after supposedly finding all this out, she'd come to his home, slept in his bed, in his arms, as if nothing had happened.

What the hell am I supposed to think?

He didn't know her at all.

"You're not the woman I thought you were."

"Harper, please." She walked toward him, reached out to him.

His heart hurt. How he wanted to take her hand. He ached to pull her into his arms and hold her, to promise her he'd do anything, anything at all to make sure that look of sadness and horror never marred her beautiful face again.

But no. He'd be strong. He'd always thought she wasn't his type. Turns out his first hunch had been right.

He pulled away from her. "I'm sorry, Amber."

"Harper," Angie said, "please."

"I'll help you," he said. "I'll do what I can to get rid of Buchanan's threat. I have some information I got in confidence from a friend. It should work to hold him off, at least until you relinquish your rodeo queen crown in a few months. That'll keep the scandal at bay. After that, you can"—he gulped—"leave town if you want."

Angie whipped her hands to her hips. "Damn it, Harp! How can you be so cruel?"

"Cruel?" He thumped his fist on his father's—*his*—desk. "How do you think all this makes me feel? I thought I had finally found someone special."

"You did! Amber's special."

He looked at her, slumped in a chair, her pretty features distraught and anxious. Her face ruddy, eyes swollen, nose red and glistening. Again his heart hopped in his chest. He wanted to run to her, soothe her, tell her he'd take care of her.

"I'll take care of Buchanan. That's all I can promise for now."

"Harp—" Angie started.

Amber stood and interrupted. "It's okay, Angie. We tried."

"I'll help you, I said." Harper raked his fingers through his hair.

"You'll get Buchanan off her back," Angie said.

"Yes."

"That's not helping."

"It's all I can do right now."

Amber shook her head. "Stop it, Ang. I want to go home now."

Angie helped Amber to the door, and the two walked away.

Amber walked out of his life.

He sat at his desk with his head in his hands. How had it come to this? They'd shared such a special time last night, and all the while she'd known about this stuff in the back of her mind. Dishonesty, that's what it was. He could forgive a lot, but not dishonesty.

And did he really believe she'd had no knowledge of the photos?

He wanted to believe her. Truly he did. But it just didn't make any sense.

Drugged? Photos of her with others? Posed? Her eyes wide open?

Couldn't be.

And true or not, she should have told him last night. She'd slept with him under false pretenses.

Sadness laced his heart. He'd thought he was falling for her.

He really hadn't been her type all along.

He sat and stared into space for a few minutes and then picked up his cell phone.

"Yeah, Buchanan."

"Blake Buchanan?"

"Yeah that's right. Who's this?"

"Harper Bay."

"Bay? How's it going?"

"This isn't a social call, Buchanan."

"What's up? Don't tell me—your girlfriend's been telling you lies about me."

"First, she's not my girlfriend, and second, I'm pretty damn sure she's not lying."

"What's she saying?"

"That you're blackmailing her."

"See what I mean? That's a total lie."

God, what a piece of filth. Harper wanted to blast through the phone and beat the shit out of him. "Buchanan, I was not born yesterday. I happen to know why you need money."

"I don't know what you're talking about."

"Stop singing that tune, Buchanan. It is so old and tired, and so am I."

"Where'd you get your so-called information?"

"I have friends in high places. That's all I'm saying. I can guarantee the accuracy of my information. Does the name Paul Donetto ring a bell?"

Nothing but static on the line.

"You still there?"

A pause. Then, "Yes. What do you want?"

"Me? Nothin' at all. But Amber, she wants to be left alone to live her life. That's not asking too much, is it?"

"Man, I need money."

"I'm sure you do. But you've obviously mistaken me for someone who gives a damn about your sorry ass."

"You want to give me the money then?"

Harper laughed into the phone. "You have balls, I'll give you that."

"Let's just say I don't give a rat's ass who gives me the money, but if I don't get it, Miss Cross's photos will be common knowledge to every person in Bakersville."

Red rage poured through Harper's veins. "You do know I could have you arrested for extortion, don't you?"

"Where's your proof?"

"You've admitted it to me. And to Amber."

"Have me arrested, and the result will be the same. Lovely Amber is exposed. Literally."

"You really have no idea who you're dealing with, do you? Do you think I was born yesterday?"

"You're a farm boy, Bay."

"A farm boy who's also a licensed attorney. A licensed

attorney who has no qualms about kicking your ass."

No response.

Harper continued, "So let's get something straight. You give the lady any more grief, and I'll personally see to it that Paul Donetto gets a first class ticket to Bakersville. But you don't have to worry about him breaking your legs."

"Oh? Why's that?"

"'Cause I'll have beaten him to it."

★ ★ ★

Amber had hated to do it, but she borrowed a couple grand from Angie. She had to get out of town. Paying off Blake Buchanan wouldn't solve her problem. It was a pain reliever, not a cure. She needed to go to the source.

It was most likely a lost cause, but she had to try.

"This is it," she said to the cab driver.

He stopped in front of the cracker box house with chipped gray paint. The lawn was dead, and a chain link fence surrounded the front yard. Trash littered the dead grass. A trike sat on the sidewalk outside the house.

Amber counted out some bills and handed them to the driver. "Thanks," she said.

"Much obliged." He got out of the cab and pulled her suitcase out of the trunk. "There you are, miss."

Amber nodded, took her bag, and walked to the front door. She took a deep breath and knocked.

Knocked again. And a third time.

Finally the door opened. A woman in a housecoat stood before her, cigarette dangling from the fingers of her left hand. Her lips were cracked and painted red, and her light blond hair was in disarray around a face that might have been pretty if it hadn't been so hard. Heavy-lidded blue eyes gazed at her.

Amber exhaled. "Hello, Mama."

CHAPTER THIRTEEN

"What do you want?"

Amber gritted her teeth. "Nice to see you, too. May I come in?"

"Don't see anyone stoppin' you."

Karen Hedstrom looked old. Old and worn-out and tired of life. In the last six years, she'd aged twenty.

Amber walked through the open door.

"Scat," Karen said, and a cat jumped off the couch. Karen shoved some newspapers onto the floor. "Sit on down if you want."

"Thanks." Amber sat, wondering if she should have brought some penicillin with her. At least a can of Lysol. Amazing her mother hadn't died in this dump. "How've you been, Mama?"

"How've I been? You're gone six years and that's what you ask? I been here. You wanted to know how I'm doin', you coulda stopped by before now."

Seriously? Amber shook her head. "I think you're forgetting the circumstances. You threw me out, remember?"

"That's right. I couldn't afford to keep you any longer. Be glad I didn't sell you off to one of those white slavers. I coulda gotten good money for a pretty girl like you."

White slavers? She is crazy. Or... "You're drunk."

"Well, now, there's a fuckin' surprise, huh? Your old mama's drunk."

"Let's get you sobered up. I need to talk to you. It's important."

"I haven't been sober in years, darlin'."

"Yeah, I believe that." Amber rose and went to the small kitchen. The acrid aroma of trash and cat pee met her nose. Her eyes watered. "I need a place to stay for a few days. And a car. You got one?"

"Do I look like I can afford a car? I hardly leave the house."

"What about work?"

"Got laid off two years ago. Collected unemployment, now I'm on welfare. Can barely pay the rent on this place and keep myself fed."

"But I see you have money for booze." She shook her head. "That was always the way, wasn't it?"

"Necessities come first." Karen cackled.

"Well, I can't live like this." She puttered around in the kitchen and found some coffee. Thank God Karen still had a coffee maker. Amber started a pot, grabbed a rag, and began to wipe down the counters. "You'll make yourself sick if you don't clean this place up."

"No one asked you."

"I'm staying here for a few days. I'll sleep in my old room."

"Sold your bed years ago."

"Then I'll sleep on the couch." She remembered the cat and changed her mind. "Maybe I'll find a cheap motel."

"Suits me."

Unfortunately, she couldn't afford to stay at a motel, even a cheap one, and she couldn't ask Angie for more money. She had overstepped the bounds of friendship as it was. She had no idea when she'd be able to pay her friend back.

"I'll sleep in your bed then. You can have the couch."

"Just a minute—"

"I'll earn my keep, don't worry. I'm going to bleach this place from top to bottom. I can't stand the thought of you living in this filth."

"Ain't you sweet."

"Sweet? Hell no. I can't stand the sight of you, but you're still my mama. And I have some questions only you can answer."

The coffee finished brewing, and Amber poured two cups. "Here, sober up."

She took a sip of her own cup and then went to the bedroom and stripped the bed. God only knew when her mother had last changed the sheets. She started the sheets in the rickety washing machine and went back to the kitchen. Under the sink she found some cleanser and dishwashing liquid. She washed the dishes in the sink, put them away, and then started on the hard part.

"What you doin' here anyway?" Karen asked.

"Like I said, I have some questions for you. And I have some other business in town."

"Yeah? Like what?"

"Not your concern."

"Then what are the questions you have for me?"

"You sobered up yet?"

"Hell, no."

"Have some more coffee. And no more vodka. I just washed ten glasses. Tell me something. If you're laid off, why the heck do you let the house get like this?"

"Just don't care, I guess."

Amber shook her head. Her mother was a mess she'd have to deal with at some point, but she had to fix her own life first.

Amber kept one eye on Karen as she cleaned the kitchen until it shone. She went on to the living room and cleaned and vacuumed. Cleaned the cat's litter box and disinfected all the bathrooms.

After she put the sheets in the dryer, she started another load of Karen's dirty clothes.

By that time, Karen had passed out, her head plunked on the kitchen table.

Good. She'd be sober when she woke.

Amber continued cleaning. When she'd made a decent dent, she looked at her watch. Nearly five. Dinner time was approaching and she wasn't the least bit hungry. She hadn't been hungry since she'd eaten with Harper and her father.

Her father.

She had a lot of questions for Karen.

She pawed through the cupboards and found a can of noodle soup. She heated it on the stove and then woke her mother.

"Mama, I've got soup for you. And a glass of cold water."

Karen swayed her head upward. "What're you doin' here?"

"I came to town. I'm staying here a few days. Remember?"

"Yeah, yeah. You got any aspirin?"

"Sure." Amber fished in her purse and pulled out a bottle of ibuprofen. "Take these."

Karen took the pills.

"Now eat some soup."

"Need a drink."

"No drinks for now. We need to talk."

Karen sighed. "What about?"

"I want you to tell me about my father."

Her light blue eyes widened. “Your father? Shit, I haven’t thought of him in years.”

“I’m sure you haven’t.”

“His name was Morgan.”

“Morgan Cross, I know. He was a bronc buster.”

“Yeah. A champion bronc buster. Man, he was gorgeous.”

Amber had no doubt. He was handsome now, as an older gentleman. And she’d seen photos of when he was young. She could only imagine how good he’d looked to Karen.

“You have his eyes.” Karen smiled.

Had she ever seen her mother smile?

“I was workin’ as a cocktail waitress at a little place downtown. I was barely twenty-one. Thunder Morgan was in town for some publicity thing, and he came in. I’ll never forget what he ordered. A margarita with a shot of Cuervo on the side.” Karen smiled again. “As if the shot manned up the margarita. Can you imagine? Thunder Morgan drank sugary margaritas!”

Didn’t surprise Amber all that much. Angie’s husband, Rafe, drank Tequila sunrises, and he was as manly as they came. “Some men like sweet drinks. So what?”

“Hey, I didn’t bust his chops about it. Just thought it was cute. Hell, I ended up in the sack with him, didn’t I?”

“Did you?”

“If you met him and saw his eyes, you’d know the truth of that.”

I have met him. I have seen his eyes.

“So what happened?”

“A classic one-night stand is all. He left town the next day. I never saw him again.”

“Why didn’t you tell me he was Thunder Morgan?”

Karen huffed. "I didn't want you trailin' after him, tryin' to find him. Hopin' your famous daddy would fix your life. You were born to be trash, just like I was."

An anvil settled in Amber's gut. Why did Karen still get to her? Amber knew better, but still, this was her mother. No matter how old she got, how far away she went, she still wanted this woman's approval.

Time to face facts. She'd never get it.

"He could have made your life a lot easier, Mama. He could have paid child support."

"Nope. I couldn't do that."

"Why not? You were entitled to it. *We* were entitled to it."

"It's a long story, and I can't get into it right now. I need a drink."

"Damn it!" Amber pounded her fist onto the table.

"Ouch. That hurts my ears."

"I don't give a flying fuck, Mama! I've got problems of my own I need to work out, and that's why I'm here. My first problem is you. Why didn't you tell me my father was Thunder Morgan? And why didn't you tell *him* he had a daughter?"

"Damn it, Amber! You don't understand what you're talkin' about."

"I understand that I had a father, a father who never knew about me. A father who could have made both our lives easier. Now you owe me an explanation. Why didn't you go to him?"

"Because he would have killed us both!"

CHAPTER FOURTEEN

"Oh, it's you."

Harper grabbed Blake Buchanan's collar. "Where is Amber, damn it?"

"How the fuck should I know? You're crazy, man. Let me go."

He clenched his teeth, the anger for Blake and the fear for Amber settling in his gut. "You're still blackmailing her, aren't you, you piece of filth?"

"I backed off, just like I told you I would. I haven't talked to her in a few days, not since the day you called me."

"Judy says she left town. Took a leave of absence. Now where the hell is she?" Harper pushed Blake into the hotel room and down onto the bed.

"You caught me off guard, but I'll warn you, we're pretty evenly matched," Blake said, massaging his neck.

"Not as mad as I am, we aren't. Where the hell is she?"

"I told you, I haven't got a clue. What do you care anyway? You told me yourself she wasn't your girlfriend."

"She's not, but that doesn't mean I'm not concerned." Concerned? He was downright worried. Sick to his stomach worried.

I miss her.

Damned inner voice. No, he didn't miss her. He was worried. That was all.

"I can have Paul Donetto here in a couple hours. All I have

to do is say the word."

"You're bluffing," Blake said.

"You wanna take that chance?"

"Bay, I may not have a choice. I really don't know where she is. Ask your sisters. They seem pretty thick with her."

Harper shook his head. "You really are a moron, aren't you? They're the first two I asked. Either they don't know or they're not saying."

"Look, I know you're upset. I really didn't want to hurt the poor girl. I was desperate."

"Not half as desperate as you're gonna be."

"Calm down." Blake rubbed his temples. "She can't be that hard to find. If you were able to trace me to Donetto, you can easily find Amber Cross."

Harper let out a sigh. The man had a point. He'd just been so damned angry. She could have gone to San Antonio. Or she could have gone to Thunder Morgan. She might have gone to see her mother. Blake was right. She'd be easy to track.

Chad McCray knew a good PI, Larry something or other. He had no more use for Blake Buchanan. He left without another word.

Within an hour, Larry had located Amber in San Antonio.

Harper tried calling her cell. No answer. He called Catie. She hadn't heard anything from her. Not wanting to worry the new mother, he didn't elaborate.

Angie was next.

First his older sister refused to say anything. When he told her he knew she was in San Antonio though, Angie sang like a canary.

"I loaned her some money. She practically begged me. She was so distraught I couldn't say no. But I'm scared, Harp.

God knows what kind of people we're dealing with here."

He sat, silent, his heart thumping and his mind reeling. Amber.

Damn, Amber, what have you done?

"Are you there?" Angie asked.

He cleared his throat. "I'm here."

"Please help her. I have a terrible feeling about all of this."

So did he. Like someone had knifed him in the gut. "I don't know who we're dealing with either, Ang. But I know someone who does."

Blake Buchanan.

"Please, Harp. If you can't help her, find someone who can."

He nodded into the phone, knowing full well Angie couldn't see it. "I will help her, Ang. I promise."

He hung up and dialed the Bakersville Hotel. When he was connected to Blake's room, he said, "Don't talk, just listen."

"What is it now?" Blake said. "I told you I don't know where she is."

"I do. She's in San Antonio. She's obviously going to try to deal with this problem herself. I have a proposition for you."

"I'm not interested."

"I think you will be. How much are you into Donetto for?"

"Twenty grand."

Twenty grand. Pennies to Harper, but millions to someone like Amber. And Blake Buchanan.

"You come to San Antonio with me and help me get Amber out of this mess, and I'll pay off Donetto for you."

"I want that in writing."

Harper rolled his eyes at the phone. "No, you don't."

"Uh...yeah, I think I do."

"Trust me, you don't. Donetto's a criminal, you moron. Do you really want your name associated with his in writing?"

"I hadn't thought of that."

"You don't think. That's always been your problem, Buchanan. Now do we have a deal or not?"

★ ★ ★

Killed? Her mother had obviously gone crazy. That nice man she'd met at Harper's wouldn't kill anyone.

"What on earth are you talking about?"

"I'm serious. I tried to find him after you were born. When I finally got hold of him, some woman told me he wanted nothing to do with me or my bastard baby, that a baby didn't fit into his plans, and if I tried to contact him again he'd have us both killed."

Amber's skin crawled with invisible insects. Surely her mother was mistaken. Thunder Morgan? The man with her eyes? The man Harper knew and respected? The man she shared dinner with, who'd called her pretty lady?

Couldn't be.

"Did you try again?"

"Hell no! I couldn't put us in danger. Though there've been plenty of times since then that I've thought I'd be better off dead."

For an instant Amber's heart softened toward her mother. Then she remembered how the woman had kicked her out when she was barely sixteen. Thank God for Laura.

"I know you don't believe this, Amber, but I honestly did the best I could."

Amber's jaw dropped. "Seriously, Mama? You expect me

to buy that?"

"I don't expect anything." Karen sniffed. "You were better off without me, and we both know it. I did you a favor by making you leave."

Amber let out a huff. "Please. Don't say that again. You may not have been the best mother in town, but I was sheltered and fed, never physically abused. Lots of kids have it worse. You were just tired of the responsibility."

"I won't deny I was tired. Seems there hasn't been a day in my life that I haven't been exhausted. But trust me, you were better off. I wasn't lying about selling you to the white slavers."

"You're making that up."

Karen sniffed again. "Get me a tissue, will you?"

Amber grabbed a box from the counter and slid it in from of Karen.

"I swear I'm not making it up," Karen continued. "I had offers, and I knew what those folks were capable of. I had to get you out of my house. Out of danger."

Amber shook her head. "You're paranoid."

Clearly her mother needed some medical help. She wasn't functioning with a full deck. Had she ever? She was making things up. When she was younger, Amber had suspected Karen might be a little off her rocker, but she'd always had too much else on her mind in those days—like making sure they were both clean and fed. Looking back, her mother had sometimes suffered paranoid delusions. The thing about Thunder Morgan killing them both was probably no different.

It all made sense now. Her mother was not only an alcoholic. She was mentally ill. Amber hadn't understood before because she'd been too young.

In a way, she'd failed Karen.

No sense going there. She'd only been a kid. She hadn't failed Karen. And there hadn't been anyone else in their lives who could have failed her. They'd been alone.

If Karen was on welfare, she was no doubt eligible for Medicaid. Amber would see she got a physical and mental work up before she left town.

If she left town.

Bakersville held nothing for her now. Angie no longer lived there, Catie was busy with her new baby. Judy could easily replace her at the shop. And Harper? Well, he'd made it clear where he stood.

Yet staying here in San Antonio didn't feel right either. Too many memories—none of them good—haunted her.

"Come on, Mama." She stood and took her mother's arm. "Let's put you to bed." She led her to the bedroom.

"I thought you were sleeping in here."

"The couch won't kill me. I didn't see any evidence of fleas or anything."

"The bed is big. You can sleep in here too."

"It's not that big. The couch is fine. I washed all the sheets in the house earlier."

She helped her mother lie down and pulled a coverlet over her body. On a whim, she leaned down and kissed her forehead.

"'Night, Mama."

★ ★ ★

His stomach hurt like he'd been punched. A vile taste threatened in his throat.

The photos. They were like a train wreck. He didn't want to look, but he couldn't stop clicking on Blake's stupid laptop until he'd gone through all twenty-six of them.

Amber masturbating. Amber with a woman. Amber with a man's cock in her mouth.

How could he have been so wrong about this woman?

He'd wanted to believe her—believe that she'd had no knowledge of the photos ever having been taken.

But no. Clearly she was an active participant in the photos. An active participant in possibly contracting a sexually transmitted disease. Granted, she wasn't actually having sex in any of the photos, but still...

How much had she been paid? A lot, obviously. Or maybe not a lot. Maybe she liked posing.

He had no idea.

No fucking idea at all.

And damn, that bothered him. This was a woman he had some major chemistry with. A woman he liked a lot. Thought he might be able to love.

Dear Lord, I slept with her. Thank God for condoms.

He'd been right all along. She was definitely not his type.

He handed the laptop back to Blake. "That's her all right."

"Told you. You still want to go after her?"

He nodded. He'd promised Angie, after all. And as much as he didn't want to, he couldn't stand the thought of anyone involved in this getting their hands on his Amber.

Amber. Not *his* Amber.

"Pack some stuff. Our flight leaves in four hours. We have to get to Denver."

★ ★ ★

Ugh. Had a herd of wildebeests stampeded over her back

during the night? Amber stretched. And groaned. Maybe she should have slept in with her mother after all. Though she had a hunch that bed wouldn't have been any better.

Besides, sleeping on this damn couch was nothing compared to what awaited her today.

Rachel's.

Marta.

She had nothing to bargain with, nothing to say. She still didn't even know the web site URL. She'd tried calling Blake to get it before she left town, but he hadn't picked up his phone.

She steeled herself. She had to try. She couldn't allow herself to be exploited any longer. What they were doing was illegal. She'd thought of calling the cops, but then it'd be splashed all over the news.

And the rodeo queen would fall.

To think, when she'd become rodeo queen, she thought she'd truly left her past behind her.

Think again, Amber.

Karen had no car. Amber whipped out her tablet and hoped like heck she could piggyback onto someone's Wi-Fi.

Eureka. There was an unsecured network in the area. She searched the bus schedules. Nothing convenient. She sighed. She'd have to use some of her cash to rent a car. It'd be cheaper than taking cabs everywhere. She should have done it yesterday when her flight got in, but she'd thought Karen would have a car she could use.

So much for trying to save money. Now she was out yesterday's cab fare, and she had to get to the airport to rent a damn car. The bus would be good for that at least. She could catch one in an hour.

Karen was still passed out. Amber brewed some coffee—

mental note, stop at grocery store and get some decent coffee—and ate a granola bar she'd packed in her bag. Mental note—also get decent food in the house. She'd get some money from Karen later—if she had any.

Amber took a quick shower and dressed. Still Karen had not budged. She scrawled a quick note and left it on the kitchen table where she hoped Karen would see it. Then she walked to the bus stop.

In less than two hours, she'd rented an economy car and was on her way to Rachel's.

With a giant lump in her stomach.

The hour wasn't quite noon. Would anyone even be there? Marta might. Her heart thudded. What would she say to Marta? What was the name of the other girl who had been there that night? Marta's roommate? She hadn't seen her again after that night.

But Marta—Marta was always there.

Amber knew she'd still be there, at Rachel's, feigning motherliness and making extra cash by drugging innocent girls.

Disgust—for Marta, and yes, for herself—clutched at her as she drove behind Rachel's and parked her car. If it were possible, this block on the edge of downtown looked even seedier than she remembered.

She'd dressed modestly in jeans and a high-necked blouse. Not the best idea. Texas heat sweltered in late April. Texas heat always sweltered.

What had she been thinking?

She swallowed and gathered all the courage she possessed deep in her gut. She sure as hell would need it.

She left the car, locked it, and steamed forward.

The back door was open, as usual. It was always open for the merchants who delivered food and drink.

The back hallway was dark and windowless, much like the dancers' dressing room. She walked through quickly, trying hard to gain bravery as she went.

Guess she'd have to fake it.

Two male figures emerged in the darkness. Not tall enough to be Oscar, the bouncer. Oscar would still be there. He was an institution at Rachel's. He'd been there for nearly twenty years.

Definitely male. They were talking to another man and a woman.

She slowed her walk, her heart pounding.

The images became clear.

Dear God.

Blake Buchanan. Holding the laptop containing the damning photos.

And Harper.

CHAPTER FIFTEEN

"Hi, Amber," Harper said.

"What are you doing here?" she demanded, her skin tightening. Had she been shrink-wrapped? "And why the hell did you bring him?"

"I'm here as your attorney. To help you. And he has information we need."

Amber stomped her foot. "You're not my attorney. I can't afford an attorney."

"Consider it pro bono. You need me. I can't believe you were going to come in here yourself and try to deal with this. You're in way over your head."

She couldn't argue. He was no doubt right. But she had to try. She had nothing to lose at this point. What the hell did he care? He'd already told her they were over.

She let out a breath. "I can't believe Angie betrayed my trust."

"Angie did no such thing. I hired Chad's PI friend to track you down. He found you in less than an hour."

"Must be nice to have a gargantuan bank account and hire a PI whenever you please." Yes, her tone was sardonic. She didn't care.

"Can the crap, Amber. You need both of us."

"I sure as hell don't need *him*." She pointed at Blake. "How did you convince him to come down here with you?"

"That's between him and me," Harper said. "It's not your

concern."

"I'd say it most definitely *is* my concern."

"How sweet of you to be concerned about me, darlin'." Blake lifted his lips in a saccharine smile. "But you don't need to be. I'm being very well compensated for my time."

Money again. Harper Bay and his clan could buy whatever the hell they wanted.

"You can both go home." Her voice shook a little. She steadied it. "I'll take care of myself."

"Can't. I promised Angie I'd do what I can."

"I thought you said Angie didn't betray my trust."

"She didn't. But after the PI, found you, I confronted her. She started bawlin'. Was out of her head scared for you. Said she'd loaned you some money but wished she hadn't. She begged me to come down and help you get out of whatever mess you were bound and determined to get yourself into."

Amber said nothing. What could she say? She was in way over her head, and they both knew it.

"My sister really cares about you. She considers you one of her best friends."

Amber gulped. Angie *was* a good friend. Especially in the last six months. She'd put aside her spoiled ways and become a true, caring friend.

The thought warmed her, but another thought iced the first one. Harper *didn't* care. He hadn't come on his own. He'd come for Angie.

He'd meant what he'd said earlier. He truly didn't think she was the woman he'd thought she was. They were over.

She wanted to smack herself, beat herself up for not telling him about Blake in the first place. She'd been so scared of how he would react.

For good reason. He'd reacted exactly that way.

"You've had ample time for hellos and stuff. Now you all just tell us why you're here."

Amber recognized the voice of Leon, the general manager of Rachel's. She moved forward out of the darkness.

"Hello, Amber," Leon said.

He looked the same. Tall, with dark skin and hair, dressed to the nines. Next to Leon stood none other than Marta. Also tall, but light skinned. And of course, dressed to the nines.

Amber's hands clenched into fists and her nerves skittered on end. If she were bigger and stronger, she'd take that bitch down right now.

Harper cleared his throat. "I'm an attorney from Colorado, and I represent Miss Cross. This is my...er...investigator, Blake Buchanan. We have reason to believe that someone at this establishment has been taking photos of your girls and posting them on the Internet without their knowledge or permission."

"I assure you I have no idea what you're talking about," Leon said.

"I figured as much," Harper said. "Blake?"

Blake handed Harper his laptop.

"This, I believe, is one of your girls. A Miss Laura Lee." He clicked. "Taryn Apart." He clicked again. His face visibly whitened. "And this is Ambrosia Love, otherwise known as Amber Cross."

Leon's forehead wrinkled. "I'm not aware of that web site. But the girls are of course free to pose for any photographers they want when they're not on duty here. A lot of our girls moonlight. There's good money in it."

"Amber and the other girls claim they had no knowledge of these photos ever being taken," Harper said, "and they certainly never gave permission for them to be posted."

"Like I said, this web site has no affiliation with this establishment. I've never heard of it."

Harper turned to Marta. "How about you, ma'am? Do you know anything about this?"

"Of course not." Her deep and accented voice melted over the words. "I trust you haven't found any photos of me on the site?"

"That is correct."

Amber seethed inside. Marta wouldn't sully herself, of course. She'd just sully the other girls and pocket the money.

"I'll admit to doing some posing during my time off," Marta continued, "but only for reputable agencies and sites."

The self-righteous tone nauseated Amber.

Harper let out a sigh. "You're both answering just as I suspected. Thank you for your time. I'll be in touch. Come on, you two."

Seriously? "I'm not going anywhere with you," Amber said. "And especially not with him."

"On second thought...you're right. We need to meet with some men who aren't so nice. You won't be safe." Harper handed a business card to Leon. "We'll be in touch."

He and Blake walked out the front door. Amber followed, her fists clenched, her nails digging into her palms.

"You can't control me, Harper Bay. This has everything to do with me. Neither of you give a damn about it. I'm the one emotionally invested here."

In more ways than one, but he'd never know that. Harper Bay would never know she'd been stupid enough to let herself fall in love with him. For that was what she'd done.

But that was yesterday's news. Today's news was she

wasn't the woman he thought she was. Well, news for him—he wasn't the man she'd thought he was either. That man would never give up on a woman because of her past—because of photos she hadn't even known about. And because she'd wanted to have one beautiful evening with her father and one beautiful night with her man before she faced the reality of her bleak situation.

Reality hit her like a freight train. He might never believe her about the photos.

Nope, Harper Bay was not the man she'd thought he was.

Too bad her heart couldn't accept that yet.

"Let her come along, Bay," Blake said. "She's right. It's her fight."

Harper's brow creased. "It's too dangerous."

"Damn right it's dangerous," Blake agreed. "It's dangerous for the two of us. But we're going."

"You said this guy's your friend," Harper said.

"Correction. This guy's *brother* is my friend. Lance hardly knows me and vice versa. I'd prefer to keep it that way."

"Then we'll see your friend first."

"Bernie can't help us."

"I think you're wrong about that. You got the URL and password from him. So that's where we're starting."

Amber cut in. How dare they stand there ignoring her? "Do you want to drive, or shall I?"

"Fine," Harper said. "You can come along to see Blake's friend. But once we get the web site guy's information, you can't come, Amber. I'm sorry. It's too dangerous for a woman."

"Bullshit. Like you care anyway." It was a cheap shot, but she couldn't help herself.

"Of course I care. I'm here, aren't I?"

She didn't argue. She didn't really want to talk to him anyway. At least she was going.

"I'll drive," he continued. "Amber, we need to move your car to a better neighborhood, and then we'll be on our way."

CHAPTER SIXTEEN

"Hey, Bern," Blake said.

"What're you doin' back in town?"

"Got some business to take care of." Blake shoved his way through the apartment door.

Harper was pleased. At least the asshole wasn't going to roll over and play dead. Yet, anyway.

"Meet some friends of mine. Harper, Amber, this is Bernie."

Bernie was square. Stocky and nearly as wide as he was tall. Even Amber towered over him. His apartment was a typical bachelor pad. Small and a mess.

Bernie stuck out his meaty hand. "Pleased to meet you."

Harper took his hand. Sweaty palm. "Same here."

"So what's goin' on?" Bernie asked.

"We need some information about Lance's site."

"I don't have any information, other than what I've given you—the URL and the password."

"Then we need to talk to Lance," Harper said. "He's been posting photos of models without their consent."

Bernie eyed Amber. The hair on the back of Harper's neck stood at attention. He moved between Bernie and Amber, blocking the other man's view.

"You look a little familiar, honey," Bernie said.

Was that saliva oozing in the corners of his fat mouth? Harper tensed. He seized Bernie by the collar. "You don't speak to her, you hear me? She's not your concern."

"Hold on, Bay," Blake interjected. "This doesn't need to get violent. Not at this stage."

The asshole was right. Though it pained him, Harper let Bernie go. "Where's your brother?"

"How in hell should I know?"

"Because he's your brother, you idiot."

"I have his address. That's all I can give you."

"How about his number?"

"Well, of course I have that."

"Call him. Get him over here."

"Right now? What for?"

"So we can all have a goddamned tea party. Christ!" Harper lunged for the man again, but Blake pulled him back.

"Just call him, Bern," Blake said. "This guy's a hothead."

"What is he? Some kind of enforcer?"

"Worse. He's a lawyer."

Harper eased off Bernie and turned to look at Amber. Her lips were trembling.

"Just get him over here," Harper said. "Tell him it's some kind of emergency. You need to see him."

"What for?"

"I don't know. Make something up. Tell him your mother's in the hospital."

"My mother's dead."

"Your father then. I don't give a flying fuck. Just get the bastard over here."

"I have a better chance of getting him over here for a beer than for either one of our parents."

"A beer then. Jesus Christ, just get him here."

Bernie shook his head and picked up his cell phone. "Hey,

Lance." Pause. "Can you come over? I'm havin' some trouble with my hard drive. I'll treat you to dinner." Pause. "As soon as you can. I have a deadline on a project." Pause. "Great. See you in a few."

He clicked the phone off. "About half an hour. So what now?"

Harper sat down on a couch covered in newspapers. "We wait."

A half hour later, a man even stockier and greasier than Bernie arrived. He oozed sleaziness, with slicked-back black hair and a short goatee. His beer belly flopped over too-tight jeans. If Harper had kids, he sure as hell wouldn't leave them alone with the likes of this guy.

"I didn't know it was a party," Lance said, looking around the room.

"It's not," Bernie said.

"So what's going on with your hard drive, bro?"

"Well, uh...these guys have some questions about the Rachel's site."

Lance frowned. "Who the hell are these people?"

Harper stood. "I'm an attorney from Colorado. It's come to my attention that you're posting photos of women without their permission."

"Bernie, I'll fuckin' kill you." With fists clenched, the creep turned to Harper. "I run a legitimate operation. I have model releases on file for all the photos I post."

"Yeah? Then why'd you just tell your brother you're gonna kill him?"

"Because he's an idiot. He knows that web site is nobody's business." He eyed Bernie. "Last time I give you any passwords for your own pleasure."

"So you're legit, huh?" Harper had his doubts. "Then you won't mind if we see these model releases."

"See them? You want to see them, call a cop. Get a warrant."

"How about I get Paul Donetto over here to break your legs instead?" Harper stalked forward. "We're leaving the cops out of it to protect the ladies. But hey, you want to play hard ball? It can be arranged."

Lance's square body visibly stiffened. "You know Donetto?"

"He's a personal friend." Well, not quite, but he knew the man.

Lance's eyebrows shot up.

"I also know all the cops on his payroll." That part was a bluff.

Lance's pasty complexion turned greenish-gray. He looked like he was about to lose his lunch. He turned to his brother. "Bern?"

Bernie shook his head, his face the same gray hue. "Hey, I didn't know he was a friend of Donetto's, I swear. I thought he was just worried about the web site."

"Fine. You can come and see all the model releases." Lance paced the floor of the small room. "Then will you leave me the fuck alone?"

"Sure." Harper hated lying. He was an honest man. But Lance was scum. He'd stay on his back until this was resolved.

They piled into the car and followed Lance to his place. His *nice* place. Posting porn on the web obviously paid very well.

"I work out of my home," he said, as they walked to the door.

"Damn," Blake said. "This is one nice setup."

"It's home," Lance said.

"How come you let your brother live in that shithole apartment?"

"When he brings in some dough, he can live wherever he wants. I made the cash for this place. The only person who lives here is me."

"Whatever," Harper said. He was tired of this. "Let's see the files, please."

"Right this way."

They entered the house and Lance led them to a fully finished full basement that had been turned into an office. "I keep all important documents in these filing cabinets." He gestured to the oak cabinets.

Harper could hardly believe his eyes. This was some classy set up for a guy who made a living in Internet porn. It clearly did more than just pay the bills.

"Let's have a look," he said.

Lance opened a drawer and starting leafing through files. "Here's the file on the Rachel's girls. What name are you looking for?"

Amber stepped forward. "Cross. Look for Amber Cross."

Lance sat down at his huge oak desk and starting going through the papers. "A, B, C, here we go. Amber Lynn Cross, is that the one?"

Harper glanced at Amber. Her face had whitened, and her knuckles gripped the chair in front of her. He took the paper from Lance. It was a standard model release for pornographic material. Harper shook his head. Like he'd ever seen a standard model release for pornographic material. But it looked legitimate. "There's a signature here. Is it yours?"

Amber grabbed the paper from him. Her complexion turned from white to ashen. "It looks a lot like my signature, but I swear to God, Harper, I never signed this."

Sure you didn't.

Harper growled. Who made him angrier, Amber or Lance? At the moment he wasn't sure. "Let me see that file," he said to Lance.

"I don't know. These are confidential papers—"

Harper stepped forward and grabbed the file from Lance's desk. He was sick to death of the sight of this creep.

"Do you know any of the other girls' real names?" he asked Amber.

"Only Laura Lee, my roommate. Her name is Laura Ferguson."

Harper leafed through the papers and handed one to Amber. "This her signature?"

Amber's lips trembled. "I don't know. I'm not sure I ever saw her signature. We each paid our own bills."

"Never saw a rent check or anything?"

"I...I can't remember. I'm sorry."

"See, man?" Lance rubbed his slimy goatee. "I told you I run a clean operation here."

"Were you present when any of the girls signed these?" Harper asked.

"Nope. I get the photos and the releases sent to me, and I put them up on the site."

Was it possible the creep was actually innocent? Harper shook his head. His mother'd always said, "don't judge a book by its cover."

"Get up," he said. "I need to use your computer."

"Now just wait a minute—"

Harper stalked behind the desk, seized Lance by the collar, and yanked him out of the chair. "I said get the fuck up."

Harper sat down and pulled up Microsoft Word. He typed in some standard language and hit print. When the paper came out of the printer, he glanced at it and then handed it to Amber. "Sign this. It's a revocation of the model release. Once you sign it, he has to take your photos down."

"Gladly," Amber said.

"I'll need to see the lady's identification," Lance said. "I'm runnin' a business here, after all."

Harper's ears grew warm. He was about to lose it. "For Christ's sake."

"It's okay, Harper," Amber said. "I'll show him my ID. Anything to get those pictures down." She fumbled in her purse, took out a wallet, and extracted a driver's license. "Here."

Lance looked at it and nodded.

"Satisfied?" Harper rose from the chair, took the release from Amber, and handed it to Lance. "Make two copies of this. One for me and one for the lady."

"I'll do it, bro." Bernie took the release and ambled to the copy machine across the room.

"Now get those fucking photos off the site," Harper said, "and delete every one of them from your hard drive. I also want any copies you have destroyed. Is that clear? As far as anyone's concerned those photos never existed."

"Fine, fine." Lance sat down at the computer. "This'll take a little time."

"You have ten minutes."

"Ten minutes? I'm gonna need a couple hours."

"Then I guess we wait. Have a seat, you two," he said to Blake and Amber.

Amber sat down, her body visibly shaking. "Harper?"

"What?"

"If he destroys the photos, we don't have any evidence."

Evidence? Why would she be concerned about evidence? Was it possible she'd been telling the truth about the photos all along? Harper's heart pounded. "You want to press charges?"

"Not against Lance. I think he's actually innocent. But the fact remains that I did not sign that paper, and I did not pose for those pictures. Yet the pictures are definitely of me, and that looks a lot like my signature. There's only one explanation. I was drugged by Marta and her friend. And so were the other girls."

Either she was convinced she spoke the truth, or she was one damn stubborn liar. He wasn't sure which yet, though her concern for the other girls was admirable.

"Look," Harper said, "we got you taken care of here. If we want to press this further, we have to bring in the cops, and then the whole thing goes public. Is that what you want?"

"Yes. No. Damn it, I don't know." Tears welled in Amber's eyes. "We've taken care of me, but how can I just waltz out of here knowing that other girls have been violated too? And they'll keep doing it. It's not right, Harper."

Harper's heart ached. He wanted to take her in his arms, tell her everything would be okay. But no...she was not the woman for him. Probably not, anyway. Still, she had a conscience, and she was right. Leaving the other girls, who might not know they were on the web site, was wrong.

"What do you want to do?"

"I just don't know. I want to go home. But I'm not sure I have a home anymore. I guess I need to go to my mama's. Her house is a shambles and I want to fix it up for her."

"This is the same woman who kicked you out, right?"

"Yes, I know. But she...she needs me right now. I don't think she's right in the head, Harper."

"If we take you there, will you take the rest of the day to think this through? Figure out what you want to do? Because if this woman is drugging girls, we'll need to bring in some big guns to investigate. I've got a good PI, but if he finds what he's probably going to find, we have to call the cops."

She nodded. "I understand. And I know I'll be dethroned as rodeo queen and I'll have to leave town."

Harper hoped she wasn't right. Bakersville was a nice town, but it was also a small town, and not immune to gossip and innuendo.

"Hey, look, I'm a businessman. I can't have cops sniffing around here," Lance said. "It wouldn't look good."

"Tough shit," Harper said. "In your line of work, you're bound to come across some lowlifes. This can't be news to you. You cooperate with whomever I send your way or I'll have Paul Donetto in here so fast you won't know what hit you. And you'll wish you'd chosen the cops."

Lance's greasy face whitened. Paul Donetto struck fear in him, just as he did in Blake. Harper wouldn't be surprised if Donetto already had a hand in this fiasco, though he imagined this was small potatoes next to smuggling drugs and women.

"Fine, fine. Let's just get this over with as soon as possible, okay? I got a business to run."

"I'm going to need your URLs so I can make sure the photos are taken down. They're not on any other site are they?"

"If they are, I didn't put them there. This site is for Rachel's girls only, and they serve a very elite clientele. Clients pay top dollar for access, and the site claims the photos are exclusive.

Whether they actually are? I have no idea."

"Seems we can assume they are for now," Harper said.

"So do you want them destroyed or not?" Lance said.

Harper looked at Amber. "Your call."

Her golden eyes were troubled. "I... Whoever took the photos has copies, I'm sure. Yes." Her eyes went from troubled to blazing. "Destroy the damn things."

"Good enough." Lance sat down at his computer. "They'll be history in a few hours."

"Fine," Harper said. "I'll take you at your word for now. I want to get Amber out of here. She's had enough for one day. I'll be back tomorrow for those URLs. Bernie, can you take Blake back to our hotel?"

"Sure."

"Good. I'll take our rental. Come on." He took Amber's arm and helped her up. "Let's get out of here."

CHAPTER SEVENTEEN

After picking up her car, Amber drove sullenly, Harper following her, to Karen's house. Amber had long gotten over embarrassment in front of Harper. For him to see the cracker box she'd grown up in was nothing compared to those awful photos.

So this was what her life had come to.

A father she didn't know because he wanted her mother and her dead. She still couldn't wrap her mind around that one. She'd met the man.

Photos taken of her without her knowledge or consent, and a paper with her signature on it giving permission for the horrible things to be posted.

And Harper. Harper, who'd come to her rescue, but only out of loyalty to his sister. Not out of love for her. She still wasn't the woman he'd thought she was.

"This is it," she said as he got out of his car.

His dark eyes were sunken and sad. Was he feeling sorry for her? Well, she didn't need his pity.

"You really grew up here?"

"We did okay."

"Till she kicked you out?"

Amber didn't respond. She didn't want to think about that. Right now she wanted to go inside and have a cup of tea and figure out what to do. But inside was still a shambles.

"Is your mother home?" he asked.

"Probably. She's not working. Most likely passed out somewhere."

"Let's go in and make sure she's okay."

"All right." She was no longer embarrassed by her mother either. "In fact, there's something I want to ask you about."

"What?"

"It's about my father."

"All right."

They went in and found Karen at the kitchen table. She'd actually gotten dressed in jeans and a T-shirt, and she almost looked like she'd showered.

"Hey," she said.

"Hello, Mama. This is Harper Bay."

"Nice to meet you. He your boyfriend?"

Amber's cheeks warmed. She inhaled. "Just a friend." She strode to the counter and put a pot of water on for tea. "Sit down, Harp. You want a cup?"

"Sure. Nice to meet you..."

"Karen. Nice to meet you too."

Amber put three mugs and tea bags on the table and sat down. "Harper knows Thunder Morgan."

"You do, huh?"

"Yes, ma'am. He was a friend of my father's. A good man."

Karen simply nodded.

"Don't you have anything to say, Mama?"

"About what?"

"About my father? About Thunder Morgan?"

"Why would I have anything to say about him?"

Amber pounded her fist on the table. "Because yesterday you told me he threatened to kill us both!"

Harper straightened in his chair.

Karen fidgeted with a hangnail. "Did I say that?"

"Yes, and *after* you'd sobered up."

Harper's eyebrows rose. "Thunder Morgan wouldn't hurt a flea."

"That's what I thought. I've met him. He's a nice man. Why do you think he wanted to kill us?"

Karen pushed a blond tendril of hair behind one ear. "He made it clear to me that night that this was a onetime thing. He wasn't gettin' tied down to anyone, and if I didn't want to go through with it I could back out, no hard feelins'."

"That's a nice guy, Mama, not a killer."

"Yes, he was a nice guy, or so I thought."

"Didn't he use a condom?"

"I don't remember. It was a long time ago, Amber."

"Well, whether he did or not really doesn't matter. I'm here."

Karen nodded.

"Ms. Cross?"

"Hedstrom. Cross is my daddy's name, remember?" Amber said.

"Right, I'm sorry. Ms. Hedstrom, did he make any kind of threat to you and the child at all?"

"Once Amber was born, I tried to contact him. I just wanted him to know he had a little girl. I wasn't gonna ask him for anything."

"Yeah?" Amber said. "So what happened?"

"I tracked down his number and called, and a woman answered."

"And?" Harper said. "She wasn't his wife. He never married."

"I don't know who she was. I assumed she was his wife.

Coulda been a maid. A girlfriend. All I know is she asked who I was, and when I told her my name, she said if I ever called there again both me and the little brat would end up dead."

"So whoever she was, she knew you'd had Amber and knew it was from a night with Thunder," Harper said.

"Seemed that way."

"I can't say for sure," Harper said, "but my guess is that Thunder Morgan had nothing to do with any of this. If he didn't make the threat personally, it's possible he doesn't even know you made that call."

"But she knew about the baby."

"You put his name on Amber's birth certificate. That's easy enough to track."

"Why did you put his name on the certificate, Mama?"

"'Cause he's your daddy. You deserved to know where you came from."

"But you never talked about him. Never mentioned him to me."

"I was scared to! I thought you might go out and try to find him and end up dead."

Amber reached out and touched her mother's forearm, offering her comfort the way Angie had offered it to her. Odd, but she wanted to comfort her mother. "I've met him. He didn't make that threat. I'm almost sure of it."

Harper smiled. "I can vouch for him too, ma'am. In fact, I could call him up and get him out here if you want. I think he'd be right glad to know Amber's his."

"I don't want him to see this mess," Karen said.

"Harper, no," Amber agreed. "I want to get to know him, truly I do, but not until this other...er...stuff is taken care of."

No way was she telling Karen about the photos.

"I understand," Harper said. "At any rate, Ms. Hedstrom, I'm sure we can clear this all up with Thunder Morgan."

"Well, he owes me eighteen years of back child support."

"Sixteen. You kicked me out, remember?"

"I'm afraid he doesn't owe you anything, ma'am. Unless a court ordered him to pay support and he didn't, which is not what happened. In all likelihood he didn't even know Amber existed. If you want to get anything out of him, you'll have to take him to court and get an order for back support. Are you sure he's the father? Because the judge will order a DNA test at this point."

"Harper's a lawyer, Mama."

"Oh, perfect. A lawyer." Karen twirled a piece of her hair between her fingers. "He's the father. I may look like I slept around, but I really didn't. So again, I get nothin'. Story of my life."

"You can take him to court," Harper said.

"With what? My good looks? Look at this place. You think I got a dime in my pocket, much less what you lawyers charge?"

"Mama, we'll figure this stuff out about Thunder Morgan, I promise. But not now. I have other things I need to do first."

She had to keep her heart out of it.

"Ms. Hedstrom"—Harper stood—"thank you for your time. Will you be okay here for the night?"

"Of course."

"Good. I'm taking Amber to a hotel."

"Harper—"

"No argument. You need a decent night's sleep. We have a big day tomorrow."

What a wonderful man! If only he could be hers.

Remember, he's not doing any of this for you. He's doing it for Angie. She nodded. "Okay."

"Come on, then."

She wanted to resist, really she did. But for once it felt so good to have a man take the lead, to take care of her. Especially when it was the man she'd fallen hopelessly in love with.

If only he could return her feelings. She sighed. That would never be. She'd have to settle for a man who couldn't resist doing a favor for his big sister.

Still a wonderful man, just not *her* wonderful man.

★ ★ ★

Amber took a long hot bath and wrapped herself in the luxurious fluffy robe provided by the hotel. Harper and Blake both had rooms on the same floor. Harper had told her to order room service, but she wasn't hungry. She was tired—oh, so weary—and numb.

So very numb.

She lay down on her bed, wanting to cry. Wanting to sob her heart out. The tears didn't come.

She got up, left the room, and walked across the hall. She knocked on Harper's door.

Harper answered, looking tousled and sexy in green cotton lounging pants and no shirt. His hair was wet and clung to the sides of his neck. Evening stubble had emerged on his chin.

"Amber. You okay?"

She nodded.

"What do you need?"

"I...I don't want to be alone."

He shook his head. "You can't stay here."

Her heart sank. "I'm not asking to stay here. Can I just come in for a little while? Maybe watch some TV or something? I just need to know there's another body in the room."

"I'm sorry. You have to go back to your own room." He walked through the door and grabbed her arm. "I'll walk you back."

He took the key card from her hand and slid it into her door. He opened it.

"Please, can you come in? Just for a few minutes."

"Damn it, Amber."

"I'm sorry if I'm being so needy. It's been..." *It's been what? A hell of a day? A hell of a few days? A hell of a few days from my nightmares?*

A hell of a life?

"Amber, I'm telling you, I can't come in."

"Why, Harper?"

He raked his fingers through his damp hair. "Damn it!" He pushed her through the door and followed her in, slamming it. Then he grabbed her and crushed his mouth to hers.

He tasted of Irish coffee, of salt, of wild berries. She'd never tasted anything more delicious. Who knew that was exactly what she'd been craving? Now was not the time to be coy. She opened her mouth and welcomed his tongue.

Their tongues slithered together in a kiss of wildness and passion. Of pure unadulterated need.

Need. Amber needed him. Now. So much now. But not just now.

Forever.

She stopped her thoughts. Forever would not happen for them. She knew that.

She'd take *now.*

She deepened the kiss and he followed her lead. With her tongue, she traced his teeth, his gums, the inside of his cheeks. His mouth covered hers hungrily. The kiss sent the pit of her stomach into a wild swirl. His lips were hard and searching. She wondered briefly what he might be searching for, but then could no longer wonder.

She let her body take over, let the kiss sing through her veins like a concerto. When his lips left hers she mourned the loss, but as they trailed over her cheek to her ear, nibbling on her lobe, she nearly swooned.

Oh, the sensation. The heady caress of his lips on her neck set her aflame. His lips continued their searing path across her shoulders, where his hands gently eased the robe from her body.

It fell into a heap on the floor. He cupped both of her breasts as his lips reclaimed her mouth.

She kissed him back with a hunger she'd never known. A desire. A raw need, both pure and impure.

Gently he thumbed her nipples, and they hardened into tight buds.

"Oh, baby," he said against her mouth. "God, I've missed you. I have to suck those beautiful nipples."

His lips left hers again, but instead of mourning this time, she anticipated their touch on her nipple. First he merely teased—a lick here, a tug there. The touch was light and painfully teasing. Her clit throbbed.

Dear Lord, I'll die an untimely death if he doesn't suck a nipple between his gorgeous full lips. "Please, Harper. Please."

He locked his lips around a turgid peak and sucked. Sucked. Sucked.

"Oh," she groaned. "So good."

"You're so beautiful, baby. So enticing." He wrapped his lips around the other nipple and sent her surging again.

He pushed her ever so slightly until they were against the bed. Once there, he laid her gently down. Her nipples were red and erect from his attentions, and they wanted more.

As if he read her mind, he clamped his mouth onto one again and sucked.

She writhed beneath him, her hips moving of their own accord. She was wet, she knew. She could feel the moisture between her legs. If only—

Again, he read her mind. One hand wandered downward, and he inserted a finger into her channel.

"Ah!" Her voice was breathy and husky.

"So wet, baby."

God, yes. Wet for him. For Harper. For the man she adored.

He left her breasts and returned to her mouth for a passionate kiss. Her nipples tingled against the hair of his chest. So, so good. His hard body atop hers, she thrust her hips upward, trying to take more of his finger. More of whatever he would give her this one night.

Their kiss deepened, and he added another finger. Harder and harder he thrust them into her, and wetter and wetter she became. Her sighs and moans grew louder, until...

"Yes!" she cried. The climax pushed her upward, nearly out of her own body. She writhed against his probing fingers, against his rock hard chest.

"That's right, baby," he said against her lips. "Come for me. Make it feel good."

She soared higher, the spasms inhabiting her whole body. Only one thing would complete this feeling of ecstasy.

"Harper, make love to me."

He rose slightly, pushed his lounging pants over his hips and plowed into her.

The hardness against her slick walls made her orgasm begin again. She spasmed around his cock as he pumped.

"That's it. Keep coming, baby. You feel so good." His breath puffed against her neck. Still he pumped, harder and faster, until she came yet again.

"God, baby. You're so hot." He kissed her neck, nibbled her ear lobe. "I'm coming, baby. I'm coming."

"Harper, come for me. Come in me."

"What? In you? Oh my God!"

He thrust hard, and she was so sensitive from her climaxes, she felt every single contraction of his cock.

"Mmm." She sighed and closed her eyes. So good. So good to make *him* feel good.

He pulled out of her quickly. "Goddamn!"

She opened her eyes.

He was standing by the bed, his eyes troubled.

"What is it?"

"Condom. We didn't use a condom."

Was that all? "Don't worry. I've been on the pill forever."

"Well, then, at least I don't have to worry about pregnancy."

"What else would you need—"

His meaning hit her like a freight train, knocked the wind right out of her lungs. *Disease.* With her past, he was worried about disease. She'd never slept around. She'd had two one-night stands, and she'd gotten a clean bill of health after both of them. She'd never slept with men at the club. Even in those dreaded photos she wasn't having sex.

She stood, anger raging through her. "Get out."

"Amber."

"You have nothing to worry about. I'm clean. If you don't believe me, tough shit. I know I'm clean."

"That's not—"

"You're so transparent. That's *exactly* what you were thinking. Do you think for one minute I'm the kind of person who would have unprotected sex if I knew I was a hazard to anyone? Fuck you, Harper Bay. Now *get out.*"

He said nothing more. He pulled on his pants and walked out, shutting the door behind him.

Amber curled up on her bed. All the tears that hadn't materialized earlier came now like a tropical rainstorm.

How had she let this happen? She hadn't gone to him for sex. Just some company to ease her loneliness and pain. He had initiated the sex. She should have been stronger. She shouldn't have let it happen. After all, he could never love her.

That was more apparent now than ever.

A rapping at her door interrupted her misery. She must look like hell from crying, but she put the robe back on and went to the door. If he'd come back to apologize, she'd listen. She loved him, after all.

She covered herself with the fluffy robe, pinched her cheeks, pasted a smile on her face, and opened the door.

In the doorway stood Blake Buchanan.

CHAPTER EIGHTEEN

Her nerves skittered. Every bone in her body ached to scream for Harper. Would he be able to hear her?

"Can I come in?" Blake asked.

"Absolutely not."

"Fine. I'll talk from here then."

"I can't imagine what you think we have to talk about."

He fidgeted, jamming his hands into his jeans pockets and then taking them out again. "I want to...er...apologize."

"Apologize? For making my life hell?" She shook her head. "I'm very sorry to inform you that your apology is not accepted."

"I'm sorry. Really. I was desperate, that's all."

"That's all?" Seriously? "You ruin my life and that's all?"

"I know it's no excuse. I've really fucked up. Chad and Catie were willing to give me another chance in Bakersville. So were some of the others. I even thought I might be able to work things out with Evie. But I had this debt hanging over my head, and even though I had the promise of work in town, Donetto wouldn't wait till I saved up the cash. When I recognized you—"

"You saw an opportunity, didn't you?"

He nodded, the look on his face sheepish. "Yes. I did."

Amber let out a sigh. She was tired of standing. "Are you done?"

"No. Can we talk for a few minutes?"

Her fear had subsided. What was the harm? The man obviously had no intention of leaving until he'd said his piece. "Fine. Come on in. But the door stays open."

"Works for me."

Amber pulled a chair out from the desk. "Sit down." She plunked down on the edge of the bed.

"I want to tell you something. About all the talk in town about me."

"Why tell me anything?"

"Because I truly feel bad about what I've done to you. I want you to know that I'm not such a bad guy."

She rolled her eyes. "I'm afraid that'll take a bit."

"I know that. You see, all that stuff about Evie being pregnant with my kid, it wasn't true. Evie and I never had sex."

"Look, I didn't know you then. I still don't really know Evie. This is none of my business. And I've got my own problems, thank you."

He nodded. "I know you do. And I'm sorry for my part in them. But for some reason it's important to me that you know the truth about me."

"Fine," Amber relented. "Then why did she say it was your baby?"

He shook his head. "I have no idea. It broke me up that she'd cheated on me. I was sitting around, minding my own business, trying to figure out what to do. I mean, I loved Evie with all my heart. I couldn't just walk away. Then her dad came at me with that gun. I've never been so fuckin' scared in my life. At least, up to that point. You know, before Donetto."

"So you left town."

"Hell, yes. What else could I do?"

"You could have stayed and cleared your name. Her dad

went to jail. You weren't in any more danger."

He stood and paced a few steps and sat back down. "There was nothing left for me there. The woman I loved had betrayed me. I was a mess. So I came here to San Antonio, got a job on a ranch—that's where I met Bernie; the ranch was his cousin's—hung out at Rachel's a few nights a month to blow off steam. Everything was fine, till I got mixed up with Paul Donetto."

"And why did you do that?"

"I was greedy. Plain and simple. It seemed like easy money. I was doing okay working at the ranch, but I didn't have much left over for savings. I wanted a big nest egg so I could come back here and try to work things out with Evie. I'd heard through the grapevine that she'd lost the baby and hadn't gotten married. She was working as the librarian. So I thought maybe... Anyway, all I was supposed to do was drive a small pickup and deliver some stuff to a warehouse. I had no idea what was in the truck. It had a tarp over it when I got it. And I was smart enough not to ask any questions."

"And?"

"And...some idiot in a semi blindsided me. Long story short, some of the merchandise was destroyed, and I found myself in debt twenty grand to Donetto."

"What was the merchandise?"

"Tools mostly. And some cocaine."

Drugs. Of course. "How'd you stay away from the cops?"

"I'd been told if anything happened to proceed to the drop-off point as planned as soon as possible. Since the truck was still drivable, that's what I did. Didn't stop to see what might be on the road. I didn't find out it was cocaine till later."

"You're lucky you weren't caught."

"You think I don't know that? I was damn lucky. I was also

lucky only a little of the coke was destroyed. Some leaked out of one of the bags."

"Why'd you go back to Bakersville?"

"I couldn't save any money here to pay him off. I figured I'd have a better shot back home where living expenses are less in a small town. I could find work and cheap housing on a ranch and get a payment plan going. But Donetto wanted no part of that. He wanted a lump sum. And he wanted it yesterday."

Amber nodded, her skin prickling. "Enter me."

"Yeah. That pretty much sums it up."

"If Catie hadn't told you I wanted barrel racing lessons, we never would have met. I mean, it's unlikely you'd ever come in for a manicure. Not that I'm blaming Catie. It's just...weird to think of chains of events sometimes, you know?"

"Tell me about it." He stood. "Well, now I've got that off my chest. I really am sorry."

"Have you told Harper all of this?"

"Yeah. After he agreed to pay off my debt, he said he wanted the truth and nothing but the truth. Goddamned lawyers."

Amber tried to hide her smile.

"Anyway, I wanted you to know I'm not such a bad guy. And I'm truly sorry. I really felt I had no choice."

"There's always a choice, Blake."

He closed his eyes and let out a sigh. "That's what my daddy always used to tell me."

"Your daddy was right. I had a choice too. I didn't have to work at Rachel's. I could have scrounged around until I found a job doing nails and then scraped by. But Rachel's offered good money, which was heaven for a girl like me. I grew up with nothing. I made the choice to do something I didn't really want to do for the money. And now I'm in this jam."

"You got greedy."

"Yes, I suppose I did."

"Then we're not so different after all." Blake smiled.

"I wouldn't go that far," Amber said. "I think you need to go now. I need to get some sleep."

"Yeah, me too. But look on the bright side. If I hadn't found those pics and blackmailed you, they'd still be posted without your knowledge. Someone would have recognized you eventually. Every cowpoke west of the Mississippi spends a night at Rachel's. It's kind of our birthright."

He had a point, but she wasn't quite ready to accept it yet. What he had done to her still hurt like hell.

"Good night," she said.

He left quietly.

* * *

Harper slept fitfully, a certain blonde invading his dreams whenever he drifted off. He woke up each time in a cold sweat with a raging erection.

Why couldn't he shake her?

Her reaction last night had been downright rage. She thought—no, she *knew*—she was clean.

He couldn't ever really *know* the truth. He had to choose to believe her. He had to have faith in his heart that she would not lie about this.

When his alarm went off at seven a.m., he felt like he'd spent the night in a torture chamber—physically and emotionally exhausted and in pain.

He was still lying in bed when his cell phone buzzed at seven thirty on the dot. Larry.

"What's the word, Lar?"

"I don't know a whole lot yet. I won't be able to do any thorough investigation until I come down there, but here's what I was able to uncover overnight. I was able to hack into their mainframe and the first security level. Still don't have access to the real good stuff. I can tell you that Rachel's definitely does some shady business on the side, including the web site you told me about. They've also done some smuggling. Some of their women are illegals who do more than just dance, if you get my drift."

Harper got the drift all right. "Are they in league with Donetto?"

"Not from what I can tell. In fact, it doesn't look like Donetto even knows what they're up to. If he did, he'd want his piece for sure."

Hmm. Good. Harper could use that.

"The manager, Leon, seems to be innocent. I couldn't find him associated with any of the underground dealings. The woman, Marta, is originally from Austria. She's not a U.S. citizen, but she's here legally and has a green card."

"When did she come over?"

"About ten years ago. She married a cowboy but they divorced two years later. Might have been a marriage of convenience, who knows? But it was never questioned. After her marriage failed, she found work at Rachel's."

"Can we tie her to the shady stuff?"

"Not yet. She does pose for other sites, though. I'll e-mail you the URLs."

"Okay. Thanks."

"You want some advice?" Larry asked.

"Sure. What the hell."

"Bring the cops in on this. These people are most likely dangerous."

"You just said Donetto's not involved."

"I said from what I can tell, he's not involved. Paul Donetto's not the only dangerous man in San Antonio."

Harper threw the comforter off and sat up in bed. "Point taken. Thanks, Lar."

"I won't be able to get out there for a few days. I've got stuff going on."

"Yeah, I know. I understand. Keep doing what you're doing. If you find anything new, give me a call."

"Will do."

Harper clicked off his phone, rose, and started the shower.

Amber's image popped into his mind. Amber's platinum hair falling in soft waves over her milky shoulders. Amber's full red lips, swollen from his kisses. Amber's hard nipples, pink and wanting, her skin silky smooth under his tongue.

Amber's wetness on his fingers, sweet and tangy as he brought them to his mouth.

He sighed and turned the faucet to cold.

CHAPTER NINETEEN

Friday night. They hadn't accomplished much during the day, though Amber's mother's house was now spotless. If they could sober the woman up, maybe she'd get on with her life.

Amber didn't hold out much hope for that. She did say she wanted to get her mother some help, though, so Harper had arranged a visit to a mental health and substance abuse facility. Amber was convinced her mother was mentally ill.

Amber was back at the hotel now, while Harper and Blake sat out back of Rachel's in a rental car watching the employees' entrance. Amber claimed the night she'd blacked out had been a Friday. It was a long shot, but maybe Marta and whoever else was involved might try the same thing tonight.

Blake sat in the passenger seat, snoring. Harper checked his watch. Three a.m. The club closed at two thirty. So far, only two girls had emerged from the building.

Blake let out a snort. Harper rolled his eyes. Blake wasn't such a bad guy, but Harper would never forgive him for what he'd done to Amber. He'd turned that poor woman's life upside down. She hadn't deserved that, no matter how many mistakes she'd made.

Course, Blake had made his own mistakes. Blackmailing someone to try to cover his own ass was cowardly. Blake had told him he'd apologized to Amber last night. Oddly, Amber hadn't thrown him out. While she hadn't been exactly forgiving, she did seem to understand how he'd let things get out of hand.

She understood about greed sometimes taking over.

Harper shook his head. He'd never wanted for anything in his life. What must it have been like for Amber, growing up with Karen in that rundown neighborhood? Getting kicked out at sixteen?

And Blake? He knew nothing of Blake's childhood.

Sometimes, Harper took it all for granted. He tried not to but couldn't help himself on occasion. What did he know about greed? If he wanted something, he went out and got it. Money was not an issue. If it had been, might he have made some of the choices Blake and Amber had?

The fact that he wasn't sure gnawed at him. One thing, though, had become clear as day. He hadn't been fair to Amber.

The door opened and two women emerged. He punched Blake's arm. "Wake up. A couple are coming out."

Blake opened his eyes and let out a huge yawn. "Yeah? Where?"

"By the door, genius."

Nope. Turned out to be nothing. Marta wasn't there.

"What time is it?" Blake asked.

"Three fifteen."

"They should all be out by now, shouldn't they?"

"You'd think. But"—Harper grabbed the steering wheel—"maybe we can't get them for drugging and photographing the girls. But I bet there's money exchanging hands in there for sex. I'd bet you anything."

"You're probably right, but what exactly can we do about it?"

"We can call the cops."

Blake let out a chuckle. "Are you kiddin'? The cops must know. This has been going on forever. They probably close their eyes to it."

Shit. Blake was no doubt right. If only San Antonio had a young, hot-headed detective with a conscience bigger than himself. Harper would look into that tomorrow.

The two women drove away together. Probably roommates, like Amber and Laura had been.

"This isn't working," Harper said. "I guess we should just go on back to the hotel and attempt to get a little sleep."

"Thank God," Blake said.

Harper turned on the engine. As he prepared to back out, the sliver of light from the doorway caught his eye. Wouldn't hurt to see what was what. He cut the engine.

"Now what?" Blake said.

"Check it out."

Out stepped Marta with three girls. They were laughing and walking arm in arm. They ambled to a black minivan and got in.

"Bingo," Harper said. "Looks like we're back in business."

"What're we gonna do? Follow them?"

"That's exactly what we're going to do."

"Christ, I'm exhausted."

"So am I. Quit your bitching."

"Is all this really worth the twenty grand you paid Donetto?"

Harper shook his head. What was with this guy sometimes? "Think about what you just said."

"Sorry. You're right. I owe you big time."

"That's right. Let's get going. You know the area, so I need you to keep an eye on that van. I need to stay far enough back so they don't know we're following. If we lose sight, you need to figure out which way they went based on your knowledge of the area."

"And what if I'm wrong?"

"Don't be wrong."

Harper pulled out and followed the black van. He kept a safe distance behind it and didn't lose sight.

Half an hour later, they pulled up in the parking lot of some expensive-looking townhomes.

"Damn," Blake said. "Drugging women and taking photos obviously pays pretty well."

"This is the porn industry," Harper said. "You saw Lance's digs. He certainly didn't make that kind of dough doing anything upstanding. That guy's as slimy as they come."

"I gotta admit, he's even creepier than his brother."

"Why do you hang out with him if you think he's a creep?"

"We worked on the same ranch, before he started doing his computer work. All us hands hung out on our nights off. Bernie's a good guy, just creepy looking. He can't help that."

Harper shook his head. "Of course. No such thing as eating right and working out."

He didn't give a damn who Blake Buchanan counted as his friends. All he wanted was to get to the bottom of this mess and get the hell out of Dodge. He'd had about all he could take of this fair city.

The foursome entered number three hundred. About a minute later, a large man appeared out of the shadows and entered as well. He could have been the bouncer—Amber said his name was Oscar—from Rachel's, but Harper wasn't sure in the dark. He didn't use a key, so Marta must have left the door unlocked. Harper hoped the man hadn't turned the deadbolt. If he had, they'd have to find another way in.

He turned to Blake. "You know anything about breaking

and entering?"

"Hell, no. I'm not a criminal. You know my story. Got mixed up with some bad people. I've never broken and entered in my life."

"Shit."

"So you want me to be a criminal?"

"If you were, the knowledge would come in handy right about now."

"Sorry I can't oblige."

Harper sighed and pulled out some rubber gloves from the glove compartment.

"Hey, a glove compartment with gloves," Blake said. "Ingenious."

"Ha-ha. Funny." He took two gloves out of the box and handed them to Blake. "Put these on. We sure as hell don't want our fingerprints anywhere around here."

They both donned the disposable gloves. Harper unlatched his car door, his heart pounding. "Let's go."

Blake nodded. They crept stealthily toward the door of the townhome. Harper tried the door. Locked, just as he'd feared.

Well, at least they weren't *stupid* criminals. Would've made their jobs a lot easier though.

"Let's go around to the back," Harper said.

They walked around the row of homes to the back door of the unit in question. Also locked. They looked down the basement window well, but the window was covered.

Damn.

They'd been doing this for so long, Harper had hoped they'd gotten careless. No such luck. Course if they'd gotten careless, chances are they wouldn't still be getting away with it. Amber's photos had been taken almost three years ago according to her, and still they were using the same MO.

"I was just thinking," Blake whispered.

"About what?"

"Bernie's gonna get into a hell of a lot of trouble with his brother for giving me that information about the site. Course he isn't the brightest bulb."

"I'd say he's not," Harper said. "But neither is Lance for giving the stuff to Bernie."

"True enough. Lance may be a whiz with computers, but he's got no sense when it comes to anything else."

"What does this have to do with anything?"

"How long do you think it'll take these thugs to find out Lance took down Amber's photos? They'll go to him, he'll produce that paper you wrote up, and they'll know something's up."

"And?"

"Maybe they'll take the site down themselves."

"Are you crazy? They won't take the site down. They'll off Lance. Maybe Bernie too. And they'll come after us." Harper's pulse raced. His words were true.

Blake let out long sigh. "It was just a thought. Since it doesn't look like we're getting in here tonight."

"I guess we should give it up," Harper agreed. "This place is as secure as Fort Knox." His heart fell. He'd really wanted to get something on these guys. Not for Amber, of course. They'd already gotten her photos taken down. But for all the other innocent girls.

His conscience nagged at him. *For Amber. You know it's for Amber.* She was the one who didn't want to leave the other girls exploited. He'd treated her unfairly. He had a lot to make up for.

Course it didn't matter anyway. They'd accomplished nothing.

Well, not nothing, actually. They knew the address. Likely the girls never remembered exactly where they'd been as well as not remembering what went on.

"You're right. Let's get back to the car," Blake said.

They walked to the car and got in. Harper discarded his gloves and grabbed a notepad and pen from the glove compartment. "This is number three hundred. What's this complex called?"

"We're in Peaceful Pines. It's an expensive upscale retirement community."

Harper jerked his neck around until it hurt. "A retirement community? Seriously? Why didn't you tell me that before?"

"I meant to, but we got off topic talking about how well the porn industry pays. I forgot."

"Nothing like hiding in plain sight. No one would look for a porn ring in a retirement community. They must have soundproofed the place. But how in hell did Marta get into a retirement community?"

"Duh," Blake said. "Through an elderly relative or friend. Or with fake IDs. It'd be pretty easy."

Harper nodded. "Yeah, I suppose so."

He scribbled the name of the community on his pad, shaking his head. A retirement community. Ingenious. He shoved the pad and pen back into the glove compartment and started the ignition.

As he put the car in gear, a knock on the window startled him.

He turned to face the nose of a gun—attached to a giant bear of a man.

★ ★ ★

Amber shot up in bed.

She'd had a horrible nightmare. Harper was in trouble. Huge thugs were chasing him, firing shots from long handled shotguns. He ran, huffing and puffing, sweat pouring from his brow into his eyes.

Damn! Why had he and Blake gone out investigating tonight?

She looked at the clock on her nightstand. Four a.m. Surely they were back by now, right?

She called Harper's cell number. No answer. Blake. Again no answer.

She got out of bed, wrapped herself in a robe, grabbed her key card, and walked across the hall to Harper's room and knocked.

No answer.

Blake's room.

Still no answer.

Goddamn them!

She went back to her room and paced across the floor for several minutes, her heart racing. What to do, what to do? She couldn't go out looking for them. She had no idea where to start.

Oh, yes, she did. Rachel's.

She'd start at Rachel's.

Who knew? Maybe they were still there staking out the place. The place had closed to the public an hour and a half ago, but who knew what else was going on?

She hurriedly dressed in jeans, a T-shirt, and flip-flops, ran a comb through her hair, grabbed her purse, and ran to the elevator.

Adrenaline pumped through her. All cognitive thought ceased except for two words in bold black letters that thumped in her head in time with her heartbeat.

Find Harper.

CHAPTER TWENTY

"Get out of the car now or I'll blow this lock off and drag you out myself," the man said.

Harper's heart lurched, and for a moment he thought he was going to throw up. He took a deep breath and exhaled.

"Shit," Blake said. "What do we do?"

"We get out," Harper said, his hands shaking.

Blake was fumbling with his cell phone.

"I said get the fuck out!" The gun banged on the window again.

Harper left his cell phone in the car—they'd no doubt take it from him anyway—and slowly exited the vehicle. The man frisked them both, took their wallets and Blake's cell phone.

"Move it," the man said. He marched them to the front door of the unit they'd been watching. He produced a key and opened the door. "Get inside."

"I guess we found a way to get in after all," Blake whispered.

"Jesus, shut up!" Harper hissed.

His bowels gurgled and his stomach clenched. Every nerve in his body was on edge. He walked into the townhome. The main floor was dark as midnight. What was going on? Could they have been wrong?

The gunman led them to a door and opened it. Steps to a basement appeared. "Go on down." He nudged Harper with the gun.

Harper nearly lost his footing and tumbled down the

staircase. He caught himself in time and shakily walked down the steps. Blake's breath was hot on the back of his neck.

At the bottom of the stairs stood a closed door.

"Open it," the man said.

Harper turned the knob.

Inside was a huge room decorated in early American sleaze. He recognized the red satin bed sheets Amber had been photographed on. That was the vanilla area, obviously. On the other side of the room was a stockade, whips and chains, suspension hangers from the ceiling. Every torture device he could imagine, and some he couldn't have imagined in his worst nightmares.

Three women lay on the red satin bed. Two were playing with each other, their eyes glazed over. The other was out cold. *Drugged. God help me, Amber was telling the truth. Amber. Sweet, beautiful Amber.*

Marta, clad in a black satin robe, covered the unconscious girl with a quilt.

Three cameras stood on tripods at various points throughout the room.

No doubt what was going on here.

"I found some peepers," the big man said. "Saw them nosing around out back and followed them to their car."

A bigger man—Oscar, the bouncer from Rachel's—stalked forward. "Good work, Don. Who the hell are you two?" He studied them. "Wait a minute, weren't you in the club the other day? Jesus Christ, this is that lawyer who's been skulking around asking questions. Holy fuck."

"You've got the wrong guys," Blake said. "We don't know anything about any lawyers."

"Cut the crap," Oscar said. "I don't forget a face. What the fuck do you think you're doin' here?"

Harper gulped. "Trying to stop you from harming any more innocent women."

Oscar let out a boisterous laugh. "Excuse me? We don't hurt anyone. They come here of their own free will."

"Right, and then you drug them and have them pose for pictures and make them sign their rights away. We know all about your operation."

"Jesus," Blake said through clenched teeth, "shut the fuck up, Bay."

"What does it matter now?"

Oscar clapped him on the back so hard he almost fell over. "You're absolutely right. What does it matter now? Because I'm afraid we can't let the two of you live."

"Hey, we don't know anything," Blake said, shaking. "Nothing at all."

Harper said nothing. His stomach threatened to empty. For a moment, he envisioned his brains glopped all over the gold carpeting, but then he realized these were professionals. They wouldn't make a mess of things. One bullet to the back of the head, a clean shot. What would they do with the bodies? What would happen to Amber when he and Blake didn't come back?

Weird, his life wasn't flashing before his eyes. Just his brains on the carpet.

And Amber.

Beautiful Amber.

"Take care of 'em, Don," Oscar said. "You know what to do."

"You got it, boss." He nudged Harper and then Blake with the gun. "Come on."

Harper's guts threatened to explode. He was going to be sick right here, right all over Don's ostrich boots. What would happen to their bodies? The goon had taken their wallets with their IDs. They'd be John and Jim Doe.

If they were ever found...

His bowels convulsed. Was he going to shit right here? Right in front of Blake and the thug?

He didn't give a flying fuck.

His life was over.

"Hold it right there, asshole," a deep voice said. "Take the gun off those boys. I got ten of my men upstairs and all around this place, and if you don't do what I say, I'll set fire to this whole operation."

Harper didn't dare turn around. The sound of Don's gun hitting the floor was operatic to his ears.

The next voice he heard was Oscar's. "Donetto. What are you doin' here?"

"I heard there was a party goin' on and I wasn't invited, you dumb fuck."

"Where the hell did he come from?" Harper whispered to Blake.

"I texted him."

"Are you fucking crazy?"

"Hey, Amber didn't want the cops involved. He's the next best thing."

Harper's heart still beat like a bass drum against his sternum. He was safe. He wasn't going to die. At least not yet. Five minutes felt like a lifetime reprieve.

Oscar strode forward. A head taller than Donetto, he was an imposing presence. "This has nothing to do with you."

"So? When has that stopped me from showing up

wherever I want to?" Donetto looked around. "Now what exactly is going on here? Buchanan's text said it would interest me. And I have to say, given the looks of things, I'm definitely interested."

"They're drugging girls and taking X-rated photos," Blake said.

"Shut the fuck up, asshole," Oscar said.

"*You* shut the fuck up," Donetto said. He looked at Blake. "Go on."

"They get them to sign the release form while they're drugged, and when they come out of it they don't remember anything."

"And I care about this because?"

"They're making a hell of a lot of money on the Internet. If you shut them down, you have a new clientele. You can start your own site."

"Small potatoes," Donetto said.

"Not that small," Blake said. "They charge twenty grand a year for access to the site. And they have over two thousand members."

"Forty million a year? Must be some hot babes."

"Just Rachel's girls. The men love them and they all have their favorites. It's a fantasy. If they've got the money, they're willing to pay."

"If the site brings in that kind of cash, why not just pay the girls to pose?"

Blake fidgeted next to Harper. "They won't do it. Most of the dancers are nice girls. They're just trying to make a living."

"And you know all this how?"

"My friend's brother runs the site."

"I see." Donetto cocked his gun, which was aimed at the

bouncer. "Tell me why I should let any of you shitheads live."

"We'll cut you in," Oscar said. "Jesus, Donetto. This is business. You of all people ought to understand that."

"True, it's business." He walked closer to Oscar. "I'm a businessman myself. I kind of like Buchanan's idea. I'm gonna shut you shitheads down. You're exploiting innocent babes here."

"Since when do you care about exploitation?" Oscar backed away from Donetto.

"When it's being done without my knowledge or consent. I run this area, asshole. When you didn't deal me in, you made a fatal mistake."

Three more men entered the basement and held guns on Marta, Don, and Harper and Blake.

"Hey!" Blake protested.

Donetto looked over his shoulder. "Those two are harmless. Let 'em go." He turned back to Oscar. "Toss all those cameras over here."

When the three cameras were lined up in front of Donetto, he shot them each with a silencer.

Harper grimaced at each shot.

"Now let's fire up that site of yours," he said to Oscar, "and either it comes down, or your brains will be all over the monitor."

He turned around and looked at Harper and Blake. "Damn it, I told you two to go. Don't make me think twice."

Shit. We can really go?

Harper nearly peed his pants. "Let's get out of here," he said to Blake.

"Our wallets," Blake said.

Damn. Harper had forgotten about their wallets.

Obviously Blake had been through this kind of thing before. "Who cares about the wallets? Jesus!"

Donetto turned slightly. "Christ almighty. Give them their goddamned wallets so they can get out of here!"

Don retrieved the wallets. Harper gripped his with white knuckles as he tripped up the stairs behind Blake.

When they were out of the unit and in the parking lot, Blake doubled over and heaved. When he was finished, he looked at the ground. "Sorry about that."

Harper shook his head. "No need to be. I thought I was going to do the same thing all over that thug's boots. I've never been so scared in my whole life."

"Me neither, even when Donetto's goons threatened me. This was some serious shit. But now he owes me one."

"Huh? Why would he owe you one?"

"You paid my debt, so that wiped the slate clean. Now I clued him in on a competitor. In his circles, that's a debt. It's probably why he let us go."

"Wow." Harper shook his head. "There's a lot I don't know about the family business, I guess."

"I don't know a lot more than you, but I know a few things. They hate being indebted to anyone. The thing I know most is I never want to get involved with any of those freaks again."

"Brother, me neither." Harper raked his fingers through his hair. He checked his watch. Five fifteen. "Let's get back to the hotel. Thank goodness Amber'll still be asleep so she won't be worrying about us."

★ ★ ★

"Where the hell have you been?"

Amber had been sitting outside Harper's hotel room door for what seemed like days. When his tall, broad form walked up the hallway toward her, she jumped up and ran into his arms.

"Hold on. I'm tired as all hell. I can hardly stand, Amber."

"Where have you two been? I've been worried sick. I've been out looking for you for the last hour. I just got back."

Harper seized her shoulders. "You went out looking for us? Where? Are you insane?"

How she wanted to melt into his hard body. She held herself back. "I...I just went to Rachel's. It was dark and empty. I drove around a little. I had to do something, Harper. I was worried sick."

"Are you crazy? Jesus, Amber."

Blake let out a yawn. "Sounds like you two have a lot to talk about, so if you'll excuse me, I'm beat." He ambled to his door and let himself in.

"We're fine," he said. "But I'm beat too, Amber. Can we talk in the morning?"

"Harper, it *is* the morning."

"Not for me it ain't." He paused at the door. "I can't talk about all this right now. But come in with me?"

Amber's heart lurched. Did he mean ...? No, of course not. He looked like death warmed over. He and Blake had obviously been up all night.

But he needed her. He didn't want to be alone right now, and she knew all too well how that felt. All she'd wanted was a little company the other night, even though it had turned into more.

What went down tonight? Harper was not himself. He seemed agitated and exhausted at the same time. His eyes were glassy with a faraway look in them. It was a look of resignation, of thankfulness, laced with a little bit of...fear?

The thought niggled at her. She had been right to be worried. Something bad had gone down.

But that didn't matter right now. Harper was here, safe.

"Sure. Let's get you to bed," she said.

She followed him into the room. He plunked down on his bed, still gazing into space.

"Come on," she said, "let me help."

She pulled off his cowboy boots. Then she unbuttoned his shirt and slid it over his broad golden shoulders. Her fingers tingled as they brushed his skin.

He was so broad and manly, so incredibly handsome.

Her hands shook as she unsnapped and unzipped his jeans. The zing of his zipper rang in her ears. He lifted his hips for her as she maneuvered the jeans over his backside and pulled them off his legs.

Clad only in his boxers, he remained in his sitting position.

No hardness beckoned. He was flaccid. No matter. She wasn't after sex. She wanted only to take care of him, to nurture him. He needed her, and she wanted to be needed right now.

She pulled down the covers on the bed. "Lie down, Harper."

She gently eased him into a supine position. His head hit the pillow and his glazed eyes closed.

"That's it," she said. "Sleep now."

She took off her jeans and put his lounging pants on. They were way too big, but way more comfortable than jeans for sleeping. She unsnapped her bra under her shirt and took it off, leaving the shirt on. Then she climbed in next to Harper and snuggled against his hard body.

"Amber." His deep voice, barely more than a whisper,

resonated against the walls of the quiet room. Dawn was breaking, and a sliver of light burst through the line in the curtains.

"I'm here," she whispered against his neck.

His head turned slightly and his lips touched the top of her head. "My baby."

She smiled against his hard body. Within a few minutes, his breathing had steadied, and she knew he'd fallen asleep.

"Sleep, my love," she whispered to him. "Sleep all your cares away." She closed her own eyes. "I love you," she mouthed against his warm skin. "I love you so much."

★ ★ ★

Harper woke with Amber in his arms. Oh no, they hadn't! He sighed with relief. He was in his boxers, and she was fully clothed.

Thank God.

First things first. He fired up his tablet and typed in the URL for the Rachel's site. It was down. Donetto had done it. They sure owed him. Harper wasn't sure he liked being in that position. But Blake knew Donetto better than he did, and he didn't think there was anything to worry about.

Of course, the site could go back up at any time. At least they'd taken care of disposing of Amber's photos. He hoped to God Donetto had made sure the rest of the photos were trashed.

He wished he could be sure. For Amber. It was what she wanted. He regarded her lying on his bed, her platinum hair fanned on the pillow, her hands clasped together as if she were praying.

She looked like an angel.

He nudged her gently. "Wake up, Amber."

She opened her gorgeous gold eyes and yawned. "What time is it?"

Harper checked his watch. "Ten thirty a.m. Crap, I'm late. I have to pick someone up at the airport in an hour."

"Okay." Amber rubbed her eyes. "Who?"

"Your father."

CHAPTER TWENTY-ONE

During the ride to the airport, Harper told Amber about the previous night.

Amber tensed in the passenger seat. Her hand itched to reach over to Harper's, but she held it back. She couldn't believe Harper and Blake had both put themselves in such danger for her. And she hated the idea of Paul Donetto being involved. What if he came after them?

"Blake doesn't think that'll happen," Harper said when she voiced this concern. "Now that Blake's debt is paid, we're even. Sure, Donetto got us out of the mess with the others, but Blake says that was a payoff—for letting him in on what they were doing. Donetto doesn't like others impinging on what he thinks is under his control."

"What does Blake know about it?"

"I have no idea, but he knows more than I know, that's for sure. Besides, we're all going back to Bakersville. There's no debt hanging over our heads like there was for Blake. We're small potatoes to someone like Paul Donetto."

Amber should have been thrilled that her photos were gone and the web site was down. Truly, she was, but her tummy fluttered and her hands were fidgety.

They were about to pick up Thunder Morgan.

Her father.

What would he say?

Harper hadn't told him why he wanted him to come down,

just that it was important. Thunder clearly respected Harper enough to take his word for it and fly in.

Would he think *this* was important?

Would he be angry?

Would he demand a DNA test?

Would he tell Amber to stay out of his life?

Fear and uncertainty gripped her like icy fingers again. Why did Harper feel he had to do this? For her? For Karen? For himself? For Thunder?

She had no idea. He'd made it clear enough that she had no future with him. Yet here he was, taking care of her again. She'd never asked him to take care of her, so why did he do it? Maybe he thought if he got her father to take over, he'd be off the hook.

Thing is, he was never on the hook to begin with. True, she loved him, but he didn't know that. She'd never told him.

And she never would.

★ ★ ★

"Thank you for lunch, Harp," Thunder Morgan said, touching his napkin to his lips. "The small talk's been great, and it was great seeing both of you, but now I've gotta ask why you had me come down here."

Amber stiffened. *Here it comes. Now or nothing.*

Harper cleared his throat. "I'm thinking Amber should tell you."

Amber's chin dropped to the table. Seriously? He might have warned her.

"Well, pretty lady, what's goin' on?" Thunder asked.

"Um...well. I'm not sure where to start."

"Always best to start at the beginning," Thunder said.

"Yeah, I suppose so," she hedged. "Do you remember a woman named Karen Hedstrom?"

Thunder's forehead wrinkled. "Hedstrom? Can't say it rings a bell."

"She was a cocktail waitress here in San Antonio about twenty-three years ago. Very light blond hair, clear blue eyes."

Thunder's amber eyes lit up. "Karen? Ah, yes. Gorgeous thing. I remember meeting her. Never saw her again when I came through here. She must've stopped waitressing."

Amber cleared her throat. "Yeah. She did. She...uh...had a baby."

"Did she? I never knew what happened to her. I'm glad she settled down and got married."

"She didn't actually get married."

"Oh? Well, single motherhood works these days. Lots of women are doin' it."

"Yeah." Amber shrugged and looked at Harper. *Now what?*

"Go ahead," he urged. "Thunder's a good guy."

"Sure I'm a good guy. But what's that have to do with anything?"

"You see..." Amber swallowed and gathered every ounce of courage she possessed. "*I* was that baby Karen had. And you're my father."

Thunder didn't react at first. He simply stared. Second by second passed, until Amber didn't think she could bear one more, when Thunder finally spoke.

"Say what?"

There went that shrink-wrapped feeling again. Her guts would squeeze out of her skin any minute now. "You're my daddy. Your name's on my birth certificate. Morgan Cross."

"That's my name all right, but that don't mean nothin'. Karen coulda put any old name on there."

"She swears I'm yours. We can...do a DNA test if you want."

Thunder stared at her intently. "You're the spittin' image of Karen all right, except for the eyes." He kept staring. "God damn it if those aren't *my* eyes. Funny your mother named you Amber. People always tell me my eyes are amber. Did she name you after your eye color?"

"I honestly have no idea," Amber said. "I never thought about it. Aren't all babies' eyes blue when they're born anyway? They must've turned later."

"If you're truly mine, why didn't your mother contact me?"

Harper raked his fingers through his beautiful brown hair. "That's why we called you, actually," he said. "Karen told us that she tried to contact you after Amber was born, but some woman told her you'd have them both killed if she didn't leave you alone."

Thunder's golden eyes turned to saucers. "What?"

"Mama swears it's true," Amber said. "She swears she wasn't going to ask you for anything. She just wanted to let you know you had a little girl, but whoever took the call scared the hell out of her. She never tried to contact you again."

"I would never have said anything like that."

"I know," Harper said. "And Amber doesn't believe it either, do you?"

"No, of course not. I mean, I had met you. You seemed like such a nice guy."

"How old are you, darlin'?" he asked.

"I'm twenty-two."

"Well, the timing's right." Thunder scratched his head. "I wonder... I was livin' with a woman around that time. She was my assistant and she had a thing for me. We weren't involved, but she wormed herself into everything. One of her jobs was to take phones calls. She...was obsessed with me. I ended up having to get a restraining order."

"She must be the one who took Karen's call," Harper said. "I knew there had to be an explanation."

"That must be what happened. Damn it!" Thunder pounded the table with his fist. "That woman caused me more trouble. And if I missed out on a child... God damn it!"

"It's okay," Amber said. "It wasn't your fault."

Thunder's eyes glazed over. "She was a mighty fine-lookin' woman, your mother. How is she?"

Amber sighed. "She's not good, I'm afraid. She's an alcoholic, and I don't think she's right mentally. It could all be part of the alcoholism. I don't know."

"Well, were you happy? Did you have a good life?"

"My life was fine."

"Tell him the truth, Amber," Harper said. "He deserves to know."

"Yes, darlin', please. The truth."

She sighed. "The truth is I grew up in a poor neighborhood, but Mama kept me clothed and fed. I even got riding lessons from a local breeder who Mama kept house for. I loved riding..." She sighed wistfully. Those were good years. "Once the drinking got out of hand, though, times were tough. She made me leave when I was sixteen."

"Christ," Thunder said. "Go on."

"I was lucky. My friend Laura took me in and I was able to

finish high school. I learned how to do nails at the vocational high school, and I graduated with honors. Unfortunately, as soon as we graduated Laura's mom kicked us both out."

"I'm so sorry, darlin'. But you've obviously done well for yourself."

Amber didn't want to get into the whole Rachel's thing right now. She hoped Harper wouldn't bring it up.

"I've done all right. I have a good job now in a nice town."

"I'd like to see Karen," Thunder said. "If this is true, I have a lot to make up for."

"No, you don't," Amber said. "Please, I don't want you to feel that way. I'd love to be a part of your life, but I don't want you feeling guilty for not being there before. It's not fair."

"I'm sorry your life was hard," Thunder said, "but you came out wonderful. Your mama must've done a few things right."

Mama and the school of hard knocks. But Amber wasn't going to say that. "That's very sweet of you to say."

"Still, I feel responsible."

"Please don't. That's not what any of this is about. I didn't even know Harper asked you to come down here till this morning."

"That's true," Harper said. "She didn't."

"Young lady, I don't need a DNA test. Those eyes are mine. I'm sure of it. And I did have relations with your mother. One time, but as we all know, that's all it takes sometimes.

"This is all a lot to digest. One thing I missed by bein' on the road all the time was havin' a family. I especially miss it now that I'm retired. If you choose to be a part of my life, Amber, I would be honored."

Tears welled in Amber's eyes. She rose and went to her

father. He embraced her in his arms. Warmth spread over her body. She felt safe. A different kind of safe than she felt in Harper's arms.

"Daddy's here, darlin'. Daddy's here."

CHAPTER TWENTY-TWO

Harper and Blake went back to Bakersville the next day, after alerting the police about the situation with Oscar and Donetto. Hopefully they'd have a hard time starting up the operation again. The cops would keep their eyes open.

Amber said goodbye to Harper without tears, though she'd cried herself to sleep that night in her hotel room.

She stayed a few more days to take care of her mother. Thunder stayed with her. Together they got Karen admitted to a Medicaid-approved substance abuse facility where she'd receive weekly therapy for her mental issues as well.

"I'm leaving Bakersville," she told her father. "I need to be close to Mama. She needs me now."

"Leaving Bakersville? But you have friends there. A job."

"I'll have to go back in a few months for the opening ceremonies of the rodeo. I'm rodeo queen, and I have to hand the crown over. But I need to get down here now and secure a job so I can help Mama. Be here if she needs me."

"If you could do anything you wanted...anything at all, would it be manicuring?"

She shook her head. "No. That was something I could learn in high school, and I'm good at it. What I'd really love to do is ride horses."

"Well, your newfound father just happens to own a small ranch on the western slope of Colorado. What say you move there? If you need extra cash you can do nails in the city, and I have horses you can ride."

Joy spread through Amber. Living on her father's ranch and helping him run it would be a dream come true. "But Mama..."

"Once her treatment is complete, she can come to my ranch too."

She hadn't expected that. How could she turn this opportunity down? "Are you sure you have the room?"

"I've got four bedrooms and a small guest house. And I'm all alone there. You do the math."

"But this is your retirement. You don't want to be saddled with two more people."

"Darlin', I'm all alone now. I was never lonely on the road. There were more than enough people around to keep me company. Now, all I've got is a few ranch hands. It'd sure be nice to have your pretty face around."

"But I can't impose. And my mother... She's a handful."

"I'm not rollin' in gold, but I was a champion bronc buster, remember? I'm well enough off to take care of my daughter and her mother. It would please me to do so."

Tears misted in her eyes. Her father had come into her life, and he was everything a girl could want in a dad. Her mother was getting the care she needed, and hopefully she would heal so Amber could heal her relationship with her. She could ride horses. Life was finally coming around. Except for one thing.

She'd never have the man she loved.

★ ★ ★

A few days later, Amber sat in her small apartment packing boxes.

"I'm sure going to miss you," Catie said, holding Violet.

"I'm going to miss you too." Amber wrapped a mug in newspaper and placed it in a box.

"I wish things had worked out with you and Harp."

So do I.

But she didn't say it. "Oh, well, things are for the best. I'm going to get to know my daddy after all these years."

"Yeah, who'd have thought? Thunder Morgan is your daddy. That's something else."

"I know."

Amber had stopped ruminating on how different her life might have been if her father had been there when she was growing up. She had him now. That's what was important.

"I'm so sad that Violet won't grow up knowing her Auntie Amber."

"I'll be back in two months for the rodeo," Amber said. "And I'll be on the western slope. You'll come out to visit. I mean, you'll be out to visit Angie anyway. And I'll be there."

"I know," Catie said, "but it won't be the same. First Angie leaves, now you."

"We're not far away."

But Catie was in the mood to sulk, obviously. Violet got cranky and Catie nursed her. Amber taped up the last box.

"That's it," she said. "Judy's taking me to the airport tonight to catch the red-eye outta here, and the movers are coming tomorrow for my stuff. It should be on the slope in a few days." She grabbed her suitcase. "I'm all set."

"I hope you find what you're looking for on the western slope with your dad," Catie said. "And I hope things work out with your mom."

"Things'll work out one way or another," Amber said.

"They always do."

★ ★ ★

Harper paced around Chad McCray's ranch house. He hadn't known where else to turn. He'd come over to see Catie but found out from Chad that she and Violet had gone into town to help Amber finish packing up.

"She's leaving for Grand Junction tonight on the red-eye," Chad told Harper.

"Damn."

"What's goin' on with you?"

"I just...aw hell, I don't know. I don't want her to leave."

Chad shook his head. "I gotta say I'm surprised. I could swear that woman was not your type at all."

"She's not," Harper said. "Thing is, she is. She's gotten under my skin. She's been through some stuff that I can't talk about. I don't know if she's told Catie."

"About Rachel's? Yeah."

But about the web site and the photos? Probably not, and Harper didn't want to break her confidence.

"Yeah, Rachel's."

"Can't fault a girl for makin' a livin'," Chad said.

"And I don't."

"But you're havin' trouble processing the fact that you're in love with a stripper, right?"

"No. Yes. Hell, I don't have a clue. I've treated her badly, Chad. She won't want me now."

"How do you know that? And would you sit your ass down? You're gonna wear holes in my rug."

Harper plunked on the couch. *She's not the woman you*

thought she was. The voice echoed in his head.

How often he'd heard that voice. He'd been so wrong. She *was* that woman. She was strong, so strong, to have lived with her alcoholic mother, to finish school when she'd been kicked out of the house, to do what she had to do to make a living. She'd never asked another soul for anything. And she was ethical. She hadn't been satisfied to merely have her photos taken down. She'd wanted to protect the other girls as well.

He was in love. Probably had been since that first night.

"I love her," he said quietly.

Chad sat down across from him in an armchair. "Do you? Or is that you just can't resist another damsel in distress?"

"What do you mean?"

"It's kind of your MO, ain't it?"

Harper cocked his head, confused. "I have no idea what you're talking about, Chad."

"When your father died, you became the man of the family. You and you alone were the one he trusted with news of his illness. He didn't tell Catie or Angie. At that point, you began taking care of your mom and of Angie. You'd always taken care of little Catie. Well, now Catie has me. She doesn't need you looking after her anymore. Angie has Rafe. And even your mother is falling in love again. Or for the first time, near as I can tell, with your Uncle Jeff. And here you are, used to taking care of all the women in your family, with suddenly no one to take care of. Enter Miss Cross. Never mind how sweet, beautiful, and downright hot she is. She's got something else you just can't resist, Harp."

"And that is?"

"She *needs* you."

Harper paused. Could Chad possibly have a clue? He

did seem to have a propensity for taking care of women—his sisters, his mother, now Amber.

But he cared for his sisters and his mother. They were special to him. His father had taught him to care for those he loved. To man up when necessary.

It wasn't that they were damsels in distress. His sisters and his mother were all strong women.

And so was Amber.

Yes, he wanted to take care of her, but that wasn't all.

He loved her. He was knee-deep hopelessly in love with Amber Cross.

"I'm aging here," Chad said.

"You're wrong." Harper shook his head. "I'm not trying to rescue Amber. At least not just for the sake of rescuing her." He cleared his throat. "I love her, man."

A wide grin spread across Chad's face. "Then go get her, Harp."

Harper did a double take. "What? You want me to go get her? You believe I love her?"

"Sure I do. It's written all over your lovesick puppy dog face."

"Then what was all the crap about 'are you sure you're not just into her because she's some damsel in distress?'"

"I was playing the devil's advocate, you moron. Didn't they teach you that stuff at that highfalutin law school you went to?"

Harper let out a loud sigh. "I ought to let you have it, McCray."

"But you won't, because if you mess up my pretty face your baby sister'll never speak to you again."

"True that." Harper laughed.

"So what are you standin' here for? Go get her."

Harper was already gone.

★ ★ ★

Catie and Violet left, and Amber decided to walk over to Rena's for some coffee. She'd need caffeine to stay up for her late night flight.

She opened the door and Harper stormed into the small studio.

"You were going to leave me!"

Amber shuddered. His anger filled the room, as though it were a presence rather than an emotion.

"Harper? What's going on?"

"Damn you!" He paced the room, his fists clenched. "How did this happen to me? How did you get...*inside* me like this? How am I supposed to live like this?"

Harper punched his fist into the wall. Dry wall cracked with a thud, and a droplet of scarlet oozed down the white surface. He was bleeding.

Amber ached to run to him. To tell him how much she loved him, how much she wanted to be with him. Instead, she said, "Judy'll make you pay for that."

"Crap. I'm sorry. I just can't bear the thought of you leaving."

"I'm sorry, Harper. I want to get to know my father, but I never *wanted* to leave here."

"Then why are you?" He advanced, like a wolf stalking his prey. His brown eyes were feral, primal.

"It's too painful to stay here. You don't want me. I'm not the woman you thought I was."

"What?"

"You know my past now. All my sordid secrets. That last time we made love, it scared the hell out of you that we'd forgotten the condom. You thought I was"—she swallowed—"dirty." The memory cut through her like a knife.

"I'm sorry about that. I just... I've never had unprotected sex before and... Oh hell, there's no fucking excuse." He thunked his head against the wall. "I was wrong, Amber. So very wrong, and I'm sorry. I should never have doubted you."

Amber warmed. It wasn't a confession of love as she'd hoped, but it *was* an apology, and she believed it was sincere. "Thank you, Harper. I accept your apology. It means more than you know."

"But still you're leaving."

"Yes, I am."

"Why?"

"I want to get to know my father. What better way than living on his ranch?"

He sat down on a large box. "I guess I can't compete with that."

"Compete with my daddy? Why would you want to?"

"Why would I want to?"

He rose again, and she wondered if he would hit another wall. Instead he paced back and forth between boxes.

"Damn it, I ran all over the state of Texas to get you out of a jam. I found your daddy for you. I took care of your mother."

Yes, he had. But not for her. "You did all that for Angie, as a favor."

"Angie? Are you serious?" He raked his fingers through his beautifully disheveled hair that now touched his shoulders. "I love my big sister, but not enough to traipse all over God's creation after one of her friends."

She gulped. Her heart did a flip-flop. "But that's not what you said. I didn't think you wanted me. Not after—"

"Didn't want you? I tried. I tried, Amber. But you've infected me. You're like a virus inside me that my body can't shake."

A virus? Hardly the stuff of love letters. But Amber's heart was pounding. Emotion flooded her.

Run to him. Run to him.

Her feet stayed locked in place.

"I ought to take you right here." He stalked toward her, his eyes smoking. "Right here among all these boxes, on the floor, like animals."

"I—"

"I ought to make love to you so violently that you'd never even consider the idea of leaving me again."

"Harper—"

He silenced her with his kiss. A primal, ferocious kiss. A kiss that marked her. Labeled her as his.

They kissed with abandon, their lips grinding and mashing together, their tongues tangling, until finally Amber broke the suction to take a breath.

"Harper."

"Amber, God damn it, don't leave me."

"Harp—"

"I love you, baby. I love you so damn much."

Warmth flowed through her like sunshine. The blood in her veins turned to boiling honey. "You love me?"

"God, Amber, yes. I love you. You're my greatest treasure. Please don't leave me. Stay here. Stay here with me. Be my wife."

"You want to marry me?"

"Please. Please marry me." His dark eyes pleaded with hers. "I don't know what I'll do if you don't."

Amber smiled. As much as she wanted to live on her father's ranch, Harper was her true dream. She and Thunder would still get to know each other. "I guess I could marry you. I mean, it'll save a lot of walls."

Harper looked over at the drywall he'd damaged. "I'm sorry about that, baby. I'll fix it tomorrow."

"Okay. Just let me know what time you'll be by. I guess I have some unpacking to do."

"No, you don't."

"What do you mean?"

"We'll just move all this stuff over to my house."

"But Harp, I can't marry you just yet."

"Why the hell not?"

"I'm rodeo queen, remember?"

"Oh right." He smiled. "Well, the good folks of Bakersville will just have to deal with their rodeo queen living in sin." He lifted her in his strong arms. "I'm taking you home."

EPILOGUE

"Ladies and gentlemen," Mark, the rodeo emcee, announced. "Welcome to the opening ceremonies of the Bakersville Rodeo! We've got a week full of fun and adventure planned for everyone. Zach and Dusty McCray have brought back their bull, El Diablo, and are still offering that half-mil purse to anyone who can ride him for a full eight seconds. Maybe this is the year. Any of you cowboys up for the challenge?

"Our rodeo queen contest is underway, and we'll have this year's pretty ladies come out and strut their stuff in a minute. First though, please welcome last year's rodeo queen, Amber Cross. Miss Cross is escorted by her father, the one and only Thunder Morgan!"

Deafening applause echoed from the stands of the rodeo arena as Amber took the stage on her father's arm.

"Amber won't be single much longer. Next week, after she crowns our new rodeo queen, she'll become Mrs. Harper Bay!"

More thundering applause.

"Congratulations, Amber," Mark said.

"Thank you so much, Mark. I've enjoyed being your queen for a year, but I'm going to love being Mrs. Bay for the rest of my life."

"Well said, Amber. And Mr. Morgan, it's an honor to have you here at our small-town rodeo. But I understand you've been here before."

"Yup," Thunder said. "Busted broncs here fifteen years

ago and won a large purse. Thank you, Bakersville!"

Thundering applause again.

Amber and her father left the stage as Mark introduced the grand marshal of this year's parade, Chad's brother Zach McCray.

Harper was waiting for her in the wings.

"You looked beautiful out there, baby," he said.

"Thank you, kind sir."

"You know, the good people of Bakersville don't know what a favor I've done for them."

"And what might that be?"

"I let them have you for two more months when I should've marched you straight to the justice of the peace and made you mine forever."

"Next week'll be here before you know it," Amber said.

"True. And you know what'll be here even before then?"

"What's that?"

His dark eyes gleamed. "Tonight."

CONTINUE THE TEMPTATION SAGA WITH
BOOK SIX

Available Now

Keep reading for an excerpt!

CHAPTER ONE

Bakersville, Colorado, Present Day

"Ladies and gentleman," Mark, the rodeo emcee announced. "Welcome to the opening ceremonies of the Bakersville Rodeo! We've got a week full of fun and adventure planned for everyone. Zach and Dusty McCray have brought back their bull, El Diablo, and they're still offering that half-mil purse to anyone who can ride him for a full eight seconds. Maybe this is the year. Any of you cowboys up for the challenge?

"Our rodeo queen contest is underway, and we'll have this year's pretty ladies come out and strut their stuff in a minute. First, though, please welcome last year's rodeo queen, Amber Cross. Miss Cross is escorted by her father, the one and only Thunder Morgan!"

Sam stood in the McCray brothers' private box at the rodeo arena, taking care of his nephew, Sean. Deafening applause echoed from the stands. A platinum blond siren took the stage on his idol's arm.

Thunder Morgan. The best bronc buster in history, in Sam's humble opinion. He hadn't always won, but he'd always given the audience a good show. The man had style. Too bad he'd retired a few years back.

"Amber won't be single much longer. Next week, after she crowns our new rodeo queen, she'll become Mrs. Harper Bay!"

More thundering applause.

"Congratulations, Amber," Mark said.

"Thank you so much, Mark. I've enjoyed being your queen for a year, but I'm going to love being Mrs. Bay for the rest of my life."

"Well said, Amber. Mr. Morgan, it's an honor to have you here at our small-town rodeo. But I understand you've been here before."

"Yup," Thunder said. "Busted broncs here fifteen years ago and won a large purse. Thank you, Bakersville!"

Thundering applause again. Amber and her father left the stage as Mark introduced the grand marshal of this year's parade, Sam's brother-in-law, Zach McCray.

Sam stopped listening as Mark and Zach traded jibes. Zach was a good man. He took amazing care of Dusty and their son, Sean. Sam could never repay him for that, and the beauty was that Zach didn't expect repayment. He adored his wife and son.

"Hey, Sam, look who I found."

Zach turned to see his sister and a gorgeous black-haired beauty enter the box.

He gulped.

"You remember Sydney, don't you?"

Sydney Buchanan.

She hadn't changed one bit in five years, except maybe she was more beautiful.

"Of course," he said. "Hello." He held out his hand.

When she took it, sparks sizzled up his arm. Those brooding dark eyes seared into his own.

MESSAGE FROM HELEN HARDT

Dear Reader,

Thank you for reading *Treasuring Amber.* If you want to find out about my current backlist and future releases, please like my Facebook page: **www.facebook.com/HelenHardt** and join my mailing list: **www.helenhardt.com/signup**/. I often do giveaways. If you're a fan and would like to join my street team to help spread the word about my books, you can do so here: **www.facebook.com/groups/hardtandsoul**/. I regularly do awesome giveaways for my street team members.

If you enjoyed the story, please take the time to leave a review on a site like Amazon or Goodreads. I welcome all feedback.

I wish you all the best!

Helen

ALSO BY HELEN HARDT

The Sex and the Season Series:
Lily and the Duke
Rose in Bloom
Lady Alexandra's Lover
Sophie's Voice
The Perils of Patricia (Coming Soon)

The Temptation Saga:
Tempting Dusty
Teasing Annie
Taking Catie
Taming Angelina
Treasuring Amber
Trusting Sydney
Tantalizing Maria

The Steel Brothers Saga:
Craving
Obsession
Possession
Melt (Coming December 20th, 2016)
Burn (Coming February 14th, 2017)
Surrender (Coming May 16th, 2017)

Daughters of the Prairie:
The Outlaw's Angel
Lessons of the Heart
Song of the Raven

ACKNOWLEDGMENTS

I hope you all enjoyed *Treasuring Amber*!

So many people helped along the way in bringing this book to you. Celina Summers, Michele Hamner Moore, Jenny Rarden, Coreen Montagna, Kelly Shorten, David Grishman, Meredith Wild, Jonathan Mac, Kurt Vachon, Yvonne Ellis, Shayla Fereshetian—thank you all for your expertise and guidance. Eternal thanks to Waterhouse Press for the expert rebranding of the series.

And thanks most of all to you, the readers. Next, look for Dusty's brother, Sam, to return for his own story when he falls for a barrel racer with a secret in *Trusting Sydney.*

ABOUT THE AUTHOR

New York Times and *USA Today* Bestselling author Helen Hardt's passion for the written word began with the books her mother read to her at bedtime. She wrote her first story at age six and hasn't stopped since. In addition to being an award winning author of contemporary and historical romance and erotica, she's a mother, a black belt in Taekwondo, a grammar geek, an appreciator of fine red wine, and a lover of Ben and Jerry's ice cream. She writes from her home in Colorado, where she lives with her family. Helen loves to hear from readers.

Visit her here:
www.facebook.com/HelenHardt

AVAILABLE NOW FROM

HELEN HARDT

After being left at the altar, Jade Roberts seeks solace at her best friend's ranch on the Colorado western slope. Her humiliation still ripe, she doesn't expect to be attracted to her friend's reticent brother, but when the gorgeous cowboy kisses her, all bets are off.

Talon Steel is broken. Having never fully healed from a horrific childhood trauma, he simply exists, taking from women what is offered and giving nothing in return...until Jade Roberts catapults into his life. She is beautiful, sweet, and giving, and his desire for her becomes a craving he fears he'll never be able to satisfy.

Passion sizzles between the two lovers...but long-buried secrets haunt them both and may eventually tear them apart.

Visit HelenHardt.com for more information!